THE FIGURE IN THE SHADOWS

"A sequel to *The House With a Clock in Its Walls* has the same cast: orphaned Lewis; Uncle Jonathan and his neighbor Mrs. Zimmermann, both benevolent sorcerers; and Lewis's friend Rose Rita, who has all the nerve Lewis wishes he had. Lewis hopes the old coin in the trunk is an amulet. . . . It is magical, and it is evil; using it, Lewis evokes the shadowed figure of a ghost and puts himself in great danger. Again here . . . Bellairs combines effectively an aura of brooding suspense and . . . down to earth [characterization]. Smoothly contrapuntal, often amusing, and adroitly constructed and paced."
— *Bulletin of the Center for Children's Books*

"Crisp prose and well-wrought suspense maintain the story's pace. . . . An entertaining occult novel."　　　　— *Booklist*

THE FIGURE
IN THE SHADOWS

Sequel to
THE HOUSE WITH
A CLOCK IN ITS WALLS

JOHN BELLAIRS
drawings by Mercer Mayer

Puffin Books

PUFFIN BOOKS
Published by the Penguin Group
Penguin Books USA Inc., 375 Hudson Street, New York, New York 10014, U.S.A.
Penguin Books Ltd, 27 Wrights Lane, London W8 5TZ, England
Penguin Books Australia Ltd, Ringwood, Victoria, Australia
Penguin Books Canada Ltd, 10 Alcorn Avenue, Toronto, Ontario, Canada M4V 3B2
Penguin Books (N.Z.) Ltd, 182–190 Wairau Road, Auckland 10, New Zealand

Penguin Books Ltd, Registered Offices: Harmondsworth, Middlesex, England

First published in the United States of America by The Dial Press, 1975
Published in Puffin Books, 1993

9 10

Text copyright © John Bellairs, 1975
Illustrations copyright © Mercer Mayer, 1975
All rights reserved

LIBRARY OF CONGRESS CATALOGING-IN-PUBLICATION DATA
Bellairs, John.
The figure in the shadows / John Bellairs;
drawings by Mercer Mayer.   p.   cm.
"Sequel to The house with a clock in its walls."
Summary: A painfully overweight sixth-grade boy receives a magic
amulet which brings him luck, but also terrifying side effects.
ISBN 0-14-036337-8
[1. Magic — Fiction.]   I. Mayer, Mercer, 1943–   ill.   II. Title.
[PZ7.B413Fi 1993]   [Fic] — dc20   92-31362

Printed in the United States of America
Set in Janson Text No. 55

For Don Wilcox, David Walters,

and Jonathan Grandine

Friends who have been friends indeed

CHAPTER ONE

Lewis Barnavelt stood at the edge of the playground, watching the big boys fight.

It was a real battle. Tom Lutz and Dave Shellenberger were two of the big wheels that ran Lewis's school. Usually they beat up on everybody else; now they were slugging it out with each other. In a funny way, it reminded Lewis of the battles of gods and heroes that he had read about in the Classics Comics version of the *Iliad*.

"Here, see how you like that, huh?" Tom threw a handful of gravel in Dave's face. Dave charged Tom, and now the two of them were rolling over and over on the ground, kicking and clawing and screaming dirty words. Lewis saw that the fight might be coming his way, so he backed into the shadowy alley that ran between the school and the Episcopal church next door.

Normally, Lewis wouldn't have been caught within miles of a fight like this one. Lewis was fat and moon-faced. In his brown sweater and baggy corduroy trousers, he looked like a balloon ascension. At least, that's what his mean Aunt Mattie had said about him once, and the phrase "balloon ascension" had gotten stuck in Lewis's mind. His hands were soft and padded, and wouldn't develop calluses, even when he rubbed them with sandpaper. When he flexed his muscles, nothing happened. He was scared of fights, and he was scared of getting beat up.

Then what was he doing standing there watching two of the toughest kids in school slug it out? Well, the back door of the school opened onto the playground, and Rose Rita had told Lewis to meet her by the back door, and when she said something, she meant it. Rose Rita Pottinger was Lewis's best friend, and she was being kept after school for sassing Miss Haggerty, their sixth-grade teacher—Rose Rita was a year older than Lewis, but she was in the same grade, which was nice.

Lewis paced up and down in the dark alley. What was taking her so long? He was getting more and more nervous, with the fight going on nearby. What if they got tired of fighting with each other and decided to beat up on him?

"Hi, Lewis!"

Lewis jumped. Then he turned around. There was Rose Rita.

She was a good head taller than he was, and she wore glasses. Her hair was long and dark and stringy. On her head she wore a black plush beanie with an ivory stud. The beanie was covered with cartoon-character buttons, the kind you used to get in Kellogg's cereal boxes. Rose Rita wore the beanie all the time.

"Hi," said Lewis. "Did you have to do a lot of stuff?"

Rose Rita shrugged. "Oh, not much. Come on, let's get going. I want to go home first and get out of these dumb clothes."

This was typical of Rose Rita. She wore a skirt and blouse to school because she had to, but the minute she was out of school, she ran home and put on blue jeans and a sweatshirt. Rose Rita was a tomboy. She liked to do things that usually only boys wanted to do, like fishing and climbing trees and playing baseball. Lewis wasn't very good at any of these things, but he enjoyed being with Rose Rita, and she enjoyed being with him. It was September now, and they had been friends since April.

They were on their way down the alley when Rose Rita noticed the paper bag that Lewis was carrying in his left hand.

"What's in there?" she asked.

"My Sherlock Holmes hat."

"Oh." Rose Rita knew about Lewis's Sherlock Holmes hat. Lewis's uncle had given it to him as a Fourth of July present. But she still was curious. "How come you've got it in a sack?"

"I want to wear it on Main Street, but I want to make sure there won't be any kids around when I put it on."

Rose Rita stared at him. "You mean you're just gonna whip it out and put it on and then stuff it back in your bag again?"

"Yeah," said Lewis. He felt embarrassed.

Rose Rita looked more puzzled than ever. "Well, if you're so scared," she said, "why do you want to wear it on Main Street at all? There's likely to be lots of people there to stare at you."

"I know," said Lewis, stubbornly. "But I don't care if a lot of grownups see my hat. I just don't want some smart-aleck kid to steal it from me."

Rose Rita smiled sympathetically. She knew that Lewis was always being pestered by bullies. "Okay, okay," she said. "It's your hat. Come on."

They walked on down the alley and over a block to Main Street. The town that Rose Rita and Lewis lived in was a small town, and the main street was only three blocks long. On it were drug stores and ten cent stores and clothing stores and restaurants and bars. They had gotten as far as Kresge's Ten Cent Store when Lewis stopped and looked hastily around.

"Do you think it'd be okay now, Rose Rita? I don't see any kids around." He started to fumble with the top of the bag.

Rose Rita got angry. "Oh, come *on*, Lewis! This is just idiotic! Look, I have to go in here and buy some pencils and paper and stuff. Then I have to go home and change. I'll meet you at your uncle's house. Okay?"

She was gone before he could answer. Lewis felt a little mad at her, and he also felt foolish. He looked around once more. No mean kids coming. Good. He took out the hat and put it on.

It was really a very fine hat. It was green plaid with stiff visors in front and in back, and ear flaps that were tied up over the top of the hat. When Lewis put it on he felt brave and clever, like Sherlock Holmes tracking down an evildoer in the London fog. Lewis looked around again. He decided that he would wear the hat for the full three blocks, right down to the G.A.R. Hall. Nobody could do anything to him in that short a space.

Lewis walked along with his head down, watching the sidewalk as it went by. A couple of grownups turned and stared at him as he passed. He saw them out of the corner of his eye, but he tried not to notice them. It was funny how he felt two different ways about the hat: on the one hand, he was proud to be wearing it. But he felt embarrassed too. He would be glad when he got to the G.A.R. Hall.

Lewis had just passed Heemsoth's Drug Store when he heard a nasty sarcastic voice say, "Gee, I wish *I* had a hat like that!"

Lewis stopped dead in his tracks. It was Woody Mingo.

Lewis was scared to death of Woody, and he figured that even Dave Shellenberger and Tom Lutz would think twice before they took him on. It wasn't that he was big and strong. He was just a little wiry guy. But he was tough, and he carried a jacknife in his pocket. There were stories that he had actually threatened kids with it.

Lewis backed away. A chilly breath blew through his body. "Come on, Woody," he said. "I never did anything to you. Leave me alone."

Woody snickered. "Lemme see your hat," he said, holding out his hand.

"Promise to give it back?"

"Oh sure. I promise."

Lewis's heart sank. He knew what that tone of voice meant. He would never see his hat again. Lewis looked around to see if there were any grownups nearby who might help him. Nope. Not a one. This end of Main Street was as empty as it was on Sunday morning.

"Come on. Lemme see the hat." Woody sounded impatient. Lewis's eyes filled with tears. Should he run? If he did, he wouldn't get very far. Like most fat kids, Lewis couldn't run very fast. He ran out of breath in a hurry, and he got pains in his side. Woody would catch him and take the hat and pound on his shoulders till he was sore. Sadly, Lewis lifted the hat off his head. He handed it to Woody.

With that same nasty smile, Woody turned the hat over in his hands. He put it on and adjusted the brim.

"Gee, now I look just like Sherlock Holmes in the movies. Well, so long, fatso. Thanks for the hat." Woody turned and sauntered away.

Lewis stood there and watched him go. He felt sick. Tears were running down his face, and his clenched fists were trembling.

"You gimme my hat back!" Lewis yelled. "I'll tell the police on you and they'll throw you in jail for a hundred years!"

Woody never answered. He just walked slowly away, swaggering. He knew Lewis couldn't do a thing to him.

Lewis stumbled blindly down the street. He was crying hard. When he wiped his eyes and looked around, he found that he was in East End Park, a tiny park at the eastern end of Main Street. There were a few benches in the park, and a flower garden surrounded by a little iron fence. Lewis sat down on one of the benches and wiped his eyes. Then he cried some more. How come he hadn't been born strong like other kids? Why did everybody have to pick on him? It wasn't fair.

Lewis sat there on the bench for a fairly long time. Suddenly he sat up straight. He dug into his pocket and pulled out his watch. It was late! He was supposed to meet Rose Rita back at his house, because she had been invited over for dinner. Of course, she had to go home first and change her clothes. But Rose Rita was pretty speedy. She was probably sitting on his front porch right now. Lewis jumped up and started walking quickly toward home.

By the time he got to 100 High Street, where he lived, Lewis was out of breath. There, sure enough, was Rose Rita, sitting next to his uncle on the green striped glider. They were blowing bubbles.

Lewis watched as his Uncle Jonathan blew into the carved meerschaum pipe he was holding. A bubble began to form. It grew and grew until it was about the size of a grapefruit. Then it broke away from the pipe and drifted slowly across the yard toward Lewis. The bubble halted about three inches from his face and began to revolve slowly. In its curved surface Lewis saw reflected Rose Rita, the chestnut tree in the front yard, himself, the tall stone mansion where he lived, and the laughing red-bearded face of his Uncle Jonathan.

Lewis liked his Uncle Jonathan a lot. He had been living with him for a little over a year now. Before that, Lewis had lived in Milwaukee with his parents. But one night, both his father and his mother were killed in a car accident. So in the summer of 1948 Lewis had come to live with his Uncle Jonathan in the town of New Zebedee, Michigan.

The bubble popped, and Lewis felt something on his face. He put up his hand and wiped some of it away. It was shaving lather. Purple shaving lather.

Rose Rita and Jonathan laughed. This was one of Jonathan's magic tricks. He was able to do magic tricks because he was a wizard, a real live wizard with mysterious powers. Rose Rita had found out about Jonathan's wizardry at about the same time that she got to be friends with Lewis. But it didn't faze her a bit. She had taken it all in her stride. Once or twice Lewis had heard her tell Jonathan to his face that she would like him even if he wasn't a wizard.

As Lewis stood there giggling at the shaving-lather trick, he heard a familiar voice say, "Lewis! You look beautiful!"

Lewis looked up. It was Mrs. Zimmermann. She was standing in the doorway of the house, drying a dish with a lavender-colored towel. Mrs. Zimmermann lived next door, but she was practically a member of the Barnavelt family. She was a strange person. For one thing, she was crazy about the color purple. She liked anything that was purple, from the violets of early spring to maroon-colored Pontiacs. And she was a witch. Not a cruel witch with a black hat and a broom and an evil laugh, but a friendly, likable, next-door-neighbor witch. She didn't show off her magic powers as often as Jonathan did, but Lewis knew that she was a more powerful magician than his uncle was.

Lewis wiped more shaving lather off his face. "It doesn't look beautiful at all, Mrs. Zimmermann!" he yelled. "You just think it does because you like everything to be purple!"

Mrs. Zimmermann chuckled. "Well, maybe so. But it's nice all the same. Come on in and wash it off. Dinner's ready."

Lewis was just sitting down at the table when he remembered that he was supposed to be unhappy.

"Gee, I forgot all about my hat," he said.

Rose Rita looked at him. "Yeah, that's right. What happened to your hat? Did you wear it for a whole block, or what?"

Lewis stared at the tablecloth. "Woody Mingo took it."

Rose Rita stopped smiling. "I'm sorry, Lewis," she said, and she really meant it.

Jonathan heaved a deep sigh and laid down his knife and fork. "I told you not to wear it on the street, Lewis. The hat was just for playing with around the house. You know what kids are like."

"Yeah, I know," said Lewis, sadly. He stuffed some mashed potatoes into his mouth and chewed them moodily.

"It was a rotten thing to do," said Rose Rita, angrily. "Maybe if I had stayed with you it might not've happened."

Somehow this made Lewis feel worse. Boys were supposed to protect girls, and not the other way around.

"I can take care of myself," he mumbled.

The meal proceeded for several minutes in total silence. Everyone stared at his plate and munched silently. Gloom lay over the table like a mantle of fog.

Jonathan sat there staring at the tablecloth like everyone else. But, unlike them, he was thinking. He was racking his brains, trying to dream up something that would cheer them all up. Suddenly he brought his fist down on the table. Plates rattled, and the lid jumped off the sugar bowl. Everyone looked up.

"What on earth is the matter with you?" said Mrs. Zimmermann. "Did you see an ant, or what?"

"Nothing's the matter," said Jonathan, grinning. Now that he had everyone's attention, he folded his hands and stared off into space. "Lewis?" he said.

"Yes, Uncle Jonathan?"

Jonathan continued to stare into space, but his grin got wider. "How would you like to see what's inside Grampa Barnavelt's trunk?"

CHAPTER TWO

Lewis's mouth dropped open. Grampa Barnavelt's trunk
was a big heavy chest that stood locked at the foot of
Jonathan's bed. Jonathan claimed that he hadn't opened
it in over twenty years, and Lewis was always pestering
him for a chance to peek into it. Now he was going to
have that chance. He felt like jumping up and down in
his seat, and he could tell that Rose Rita was excited too.

"Oh boy, Uncle Jonathan!" Lewis cried. "Oh boy,
that'd be just great!"

"I think so too!" said Rose Rita.

"So do I," added Mrs. Zimmermann. "Seeing as how
I'm a nosy old lady who likes surprises."

"You certainly are, Frizzy Wig," said Jonathan.

"Nosy, that is. Now tell me, folks. Would you like your ice cream and cookies now, or after we open the chest? All those in favor of opening the chest now, raise their hands."

Lewis and Rose Rita started to raise their hands, but then they remembered that the cookies were Mrs. Zimmermann's. Maybe her feelings would be hurt if they voted to postpone dessert. They pulled their hands down.

Mrs. Zimmermann glared at the two of them and raised her hand. "May I speak, teacher?" she said in a whiny little voice.

"Sure. Go ahead," said Jonathan, grinning.

"If you don't go up and help me bring that chest down *right now*, I'll turn you into a wastebasket full of pencil shavings. Understand?"

"Aye, aye!" said Jonathan, saluting. He and Mrs. Zimmermann got up and went to get the trunk.

Lewis and Rose Rita wandered into the study. They stood around leafing through books and drawing pictures in the dust on the library table. Before long they heard doors slamming and a lot of banging and one loud shout (from Jonathan) followed by some muffled swearing. At last the trunk arrived. Jonathan was holding his end of it with one hand and sucking at the knuckles of his other hand, which he had skinned while trying to take the trunk around a narrow corner.

"Well, here we are!" said Mrs. Zimmermann. She set

her end of the trunk down and mopped her face with a purple handkerchief. "What did your grampa store in here, Jonathan? Cannon balls?"

"Just about," said Jonathan. "Now as soon as I can find the key . . . hmm, I wonder where it is?" Jonathan scratched his bushy red beard and stared at the ceiling.

"Oh, don't tell me you've lost it!" said Mrs. Zimmermann in exasperation.

"No, I haven't lost it. I just don't remember where it is. Half a minute." Jonathan left the room, and they heard him going back upstairs.

"I hope it isn't lost," said Lewis, who could get gloomy at a moment's notice if things weren't working out just right.

"Don't worry," said Mrs. Zimmermann. "If worse comes to worst your uncle will shoot the lock off with Grampa Barnavelt's Civil War pistol—unless of course it's locked in the trunk with everything else."

While Jonathan was upstairs hunting for the key, Lewis and Rose Rita had a chance to examine the outside of the old trunk. It had a humped lid, which made it look like a pirate chest, but it was really a steamer trunk, a kind of suitcase that people used to take with them on ocean voyages a long time ago. The trunk was made of wood, but it was covered with alligator leather. Three big strips of hammered copper had been nailed across the lid for decoration. They had turned bright green with age. The lockplate was made of copper too, and it was shaped like a baby's face. The baby's mouth was the keyhole.

After what seemed like a very long time, Jonathan returned. In his hand he held a small iron key with a cardboard tag dangling from it.

"Where was it?" asked Mrs. Zimmermann. She was trying hard to suppress a giggle.

"Where?" snapped Jonathan. "Where? Exactly where you'd expect it to be. At the bottom of a vase full of Indian head pennies." He knelt down and stuck the key in the lock. Lewis, Rose Rita, and Mrs. Zimmermann gathered behind him. The lock was stiff and rusty, so it took Jonathan several tries, but at last the key turned. Carefully, he lifted the shaky old lid.

The first thing that Lewis and Rose Rita noticed when the trunk was opened was the inside of the lid. It was covered with faded pink wallpaper, and somebody long ago—maybe a child—had pasted pictures on the paper. The pictures looked as if they had been cut from a very old-fashioned magazine. Lewis and Rose Rita looked inside the trunk. Under a thick gritty layer of dust were a number of parcels done up in newspaper and string. One was long and curved and thin. Another was flat and square. Some were just big and bulky. The newspaper was old and yellow, and some of the parcels were coming undone because the string was rotting.

Jonathan reached in and started handing parcels around.

"Here you are. One for you, Lewis, and one for you, Rose Rita, and even one for you, Pruny. And one for little me."

"Hah," said Mrs. Zimmermann, as she tugged at a piece of string. "I'll bet you saved the best one for yourself."

Lewis had the long curved parcel. When he had ripped the paper off one end, he saw the tarnished brass hilt of a sword. "Oh boy!" he said. "A real sword!" He ripped the rest of the paper off and started swinging the sword around. Fortunately, it was still in its sheath.

"Have at thee for a foul faytour!" he shouted, lunging at Rose Rita with the sword.

"Hey, Sir Ector, watch it, will you?" said Jonathan. Lewis stopped and looked sheepish. Then everybody, including Lewis, laughed.

"You might have known what would happen when you put a sword in the hands of an eleven-year-old boy," said Mrs. Zimmermann. "Here, let me see it."

Lewis handed the sword to Mrs. Zimmermann. Tugging gently, she eased it halfway out of its scabbard. The tarnished blade flashed dimly in the lamplight.

"Whose sword was it?" asked Lewis.

"Grampa Barnavelt's," said Jonathan. "It's a cavalry saber—you can tell because it's curved and quite heavy. Put it back in the sheath, Florence. Knives make me nervous."

Lewis knew a little bit about Grampa Barnavelt. He had seen his name on the Civil War Memorial, and Jonathan had told him a few stories about the old man, but these stories had merely whetted Lewis's appetite.

"Grampa Barnavelt was a lancer, wasn't he?" asked Lewis.

"That's right," said Jonathan. "Rose Rita, open your package."

Rose Rita was holding a soft little parcel. When she had popped the string and ripped off the paper, she found that she was holding a pile of old clothes. On top was a blue shirt that had been folded up so long it wouldn't come unfolded. Under that was a pair of baggy red pantaloons and a flattened red felt cap with FIFTH MICHIGAN FIRE ZOUAVE LANCERS embroidered on it in gold thread.

"What are the Fifth Michigan . . . whatever they are?" asked Rose Rita.

"Idiots," snapped Mrs. Zimmermann. "Idiots they were, the whole bunch of them."

"That's true," said Jonathan, stroking his beard. "But that is probably not the answer Rose Rita wanted. In the first place . . . well, let's let Lewis answer this. He's read about lancers."

"Lancers are cavalry soldiers with long spears," Lewis explained. "They used the spears to run the enemy soldiers through."

"If they got close enough," said Jonathan. "You see, Rose Rita, lancers were sort of a holdover from the

Middle Ages, when knights used to knock each other off horses with spears. But in the Civil War, lancers had to charge against soldiers who had muskets and rifles and cannons."

"That sounds kind of dumb," said Rose Rita. "How come they wanted to do that?"

"Well, I'm not quite sure," said Jonathan, "but I think they had some idea that those long spears and flapping pennants and bright-colored uniforms would throw terror into the foot soldiers of the enemy."

"Did they?" asked Lewis.

Jonathan looked confused. "Did they what?"

"Strike terror into the enemy."

"Oh. Well, yes, sometimes they did. But more often than not the soldiers with muskets and rifles cut the lancers to pieces. That is what happened at the Battle of Spotsylvania Court House. The Fifth Michigan charged, and it got wiped out. Only Grampa Barnavelt and a man named Walter Finzer came back alive. And they survived because they never got into the battle."

Lewis's face fell. He had imagined his great-grandfather slashing and lancing and thrusting his way right through the enemy lines. "How come he didn't get into the battle?" he asked.

"Go ahead, Jonathan. Tell them," said Mrs. Zimmermann, grinning. She had heard the story a thousand times, but it still tickled her.

"Well, it's like this," said Jonathan. He coughed, folded his arms, and settled back into his storytelling pose. "Your great-grampa, Lewis, was not one of the bravest men in the world. I think he joined the Michigan Lancers because he thought their uniforms were pretty. But the closer he came to an actual fight, the more scared he got. The Battle of Spotsylvania was going to be his first taste of real combat. Well now. On the night before the battle, Grampa was playing poker by the campfire with some other members of the company, and he found that he was holding a very good hand. I think it was a full house or four of a kind or something like that. Anyway, before long, only Grampa and Walter Finzer were left in the game. Walter was a New Zebedee boy too, and he had joined up at about the same time as Grampa. Well, Walter raised Grampa and Grampa raised Walter, and before long the two of them had thrown every cent they had, and their swords and pistols, into the pot. But when Grampa took off his gold signet ring and tossed it in, Walter didn't have anything to answer it with. Walter tried to borrow money from some of the other men, but they all thought Walter was a deadbeat, and they wouldn't lend him a cent. Walter was about ready to throw in his cards and let Grampa take the pot, when Grampa said, 'How about your lucky piece?' "

"Lucky piece?" said Lewis.

"Yes. You see, Grampa had gotten into the game hoping that he would be able to relieve Walter of the lucky coin he carried. I know it sounds silly, but Grampa was convinced that Walter's lucky coin would get him through the battle without a scratch. Who knows why Grampa thought this? Pilots trust to baby booties and rabbits' feet. Grampa had heard Walter bragging about this coin, so he figured that maybe it would help him." Jonathan smiled sadly. "I think Grampa was so scared he would have trusted to anything to see him through the next day's battle."

"Was it magic?" asked Rose Rita. "The coin, I mean."

Jonathan chuckled. "No, I'm afraid not. But Grampa thought it was, and that's the important thing. To go on with the story, he told Walter to throw the coin in, and Walter refused. Walter was a bullheaded and rather stupid sort, and he didn't want to part with the coin. Finally, though, his friends persuaded him to throw it in. Then Walter and Grampa both showed their hands, and Grampa won. Walter was furious. He screamed and yelled and stomped and swore, and in the end, when Grampa started to rake in the money, he grabbed a pistol out of somebody's holster and shot Grampa in the leg."

"That's awful!" said Rose Rita. "Did Grampa Barnavelt die?"

"No, but the wound put him out of commission for a

long while. Walter, of course, was put under arrest immediately, and later on he got a dishonorable discharge from the Army. He might have gotten worse, but Grampa pleaded for clemency for him. You see, Grampa Barnavelt was really a rather soft-hearted and gentle man. He had no business trying to fight in a war."

Jonathan settled back in his chair and lighted his pipe. Mrs. Zimmermann and Lewis went out to the kitchen, and came back with chocolate-chip cookies and ice cream. Suddenly, as everyone was eating, Lewis looked up and said, "Did Grampa keep the coin? Is it still around?"

Jonathan laughed. "He sure did keep it! He put it on his watch chain and told everybody he met how he got it. I got so tired of hearing that story when I was a kid."

"Could we see it?" Lewis asked.

Jonathan looked startled. "See it? Well, I guess so, if I can find it. I imagine it's rattling around in this old trunk somewhere. Wouldn't you think so, Florence?"

"How would I know? It's your trunk. Let's have a look."

Jonathan, Mrs. Zimmermann, Lewis, and Rose Rita gathered around the old chest and started lifting out parcels and unwrapping them. There was a top hat and a black frock coat shiny at the elbows, and some books and three or four albums full of old photos, and one genuine cannon ball. Finally everything was out of the chest but the dust and the dead insects at the bottom. Everything, that is, except one small battered wooden box.

"I'll bet it's in there," said Lewis.

"I wouldn't count on it," said Jonathan. "But let's have a peek anyway."

He reached in and lifted the box out. There was no lock on it, and after a little tugging the lid came off, hinges and all. Inside were an old pair of rimless spectacles, a blackened tobacco pipe, and a heavy braided watch chain. A tiny silver coin was attached to the chain.

"Hey, it's really there!" Lewis reached into the box and carefully lifted the watch chain out. He handled it as if it were a string of diamonds. Now he and Rose Rita were examining the coin. It was a strange-looking thing, smaller and thinner than a dime. On one side was a Roman numeral III. On the other was a six-pointed star with a striped shield inside it. "United States of America" was printed around the outside of the star, and under the bottom point of the star was a date: 1859.

"What is it?" asked Lewis. He had never seen a coin like it in his life.

"It's a United States three-cent piece," said Mrs. Zimmermann. "Anyone ought to be able to see that."

Rose Rita laughed. "Oh, come on, Mrs. Zimmermann!

You're always kidding. You mean this coin was worth three cents way back then?"

"It certainly was. It's worth a little bit more now, because it's old, but it's not very rare as coins go."

"Why did they have three-cent coins?" asked Lewis. "Wouldn't it have been easier to just use three pennies?"

"You'll have to ask the United States Mint why they had three-cent pieces," said Jonathan. "At one time they had half cents and two-cent pieces and half dimes and all sorts of weird denominations. So, as Mrs. Zimmermann says, this coin is not so strange—except for the fact that it's part of the story I just told you."

Lewis looked at the coin and imagined it lying on a heap of money and swords and pistols in the red light of a campfire. He imagined Walter Finzer pulling a gun and shooting Grampa Barnavelt. Blood had been shed because of that coin. Lewis had read a lot, and he knew stories about kings who had fought and killed each other over small objects. Small objects like crowns and jewels and pieces of gold. The coin seemed to Lewis like something straight out of those old tales.

Lewis looked up at his Uncle Jonathan. "Uncle Jonathan, are you *sure* this coin isn't magic?"

"Sure as sure can be, Lewis. But just to set your mind at ease, why don't you give to to Mrs. Zimmermann for a minute? She knows all about magic amulets and talismans and things of that kind, and I think she could probably tell just by the feel of the thing. Couldn't you, Florence?"

"Yes, I could. At my final exam at the University of Göttingen, when I was getting my doctor's degree in Magic, I had to tell if certain objects were enchanted or not just by feeling them with my fingers. Here, let me see it."

Lewis handed the coin to Mrs. Zimmermann. She rubbed it back and forth between her fingers and stared at it thoughtfully for a few minutes. Then she handed it back to Lewis.

"Sorry, Lewis," she said, shaking her head. "It just feels like a hunk of metal. If it was magic, it would . . . well, it would kind of *tingle* in my hand. But there's nothing there. It's just an old coin."

Lewis held the coin up and looked at it sadly. Then he turned to Jonathan and said, "Can I keep it?"

Jonathan blinked absent-mindedly. "Hm?"

"I said, can I keep it?"

"Can you . . . ? Oh. Oh, sure. Go ahead. It's yours. Keep it as a souvenir of the Civil War." Jonathan patted Lewis on the shoulder and smiled.

Late that night, when Rose Rita and Mrs. Zimmermann had gone home and Jonathan had gone to bed, Lewis sat on the edge of his bed looking at the coin. It was too bad it wasn't magic. If it had been, it might've turned out to be one of those amulets that made you brave and strong and protected you from your enemies. Like the pin that an ancient king of Ireland wore in his shirt when he went into battle. As long as he kept the pin on, he couldn't be wounded. Lewis liked that story. He had never gone into battle with sword and shield, but he had gotten into a few fist fights, and he had always lost them. Maybe if he had had an amulet, he would have won those fights. Maybe if he had had an amulet, Woody Mingo would not have been able to steal his hat.

Oh well, thought Lewis, that's the way it goes. He put the coin in the drawer of his bedside table, turned out the light, and went to bed.

Lewis went to bed, but he didn't go to sleep. He lay there tossing and turning and thinking about Woody and the Sherlock Holmes hat and Grampa Barnavelt and Walter Finzer and the three-cent piece. After that he just lay there and listened to the sounds of the house: the clock ticking, the bathtub faucet dripping, the various cracks and creaks and snaps that a big old house makes when it is settling itself for the night.

Flip-flop. Lewis sat up straight in his bed. He knew that sound. He knew it very well—but it was not a nighttime sound. It was the sound of the mail slot.

The front door of Lewis's house had a slot in it for mail. The slot had a hinged metal cover over it, and when the mailman lifted the cover to slide letters in, the cover went flip-flop. Lewis and his uncle both loved to get mail, and no matter where they were in the house, when they heard the flip-flop sound, they came running. The mailman on their route was very talkative, and so he seldom got to their house before two-thirty in the afternoon. But as far as Lewis knew, the mail had never arrived at midnight.

Lewis sat there wondering for a few minutes. Then he got out of bed, put on his slippers and bathrobe, and padded downstairs to the front hall. There on the floor, just below the mail slot, lay a postcard.

Lewis picked the card up and carried it over to the hall window. The gray light of a full moon was streaming in. It was bright enough to read by—but there was nothing to read. The card was blank.

Lewis began to feel creepy. What kind of a message was this? He turned the card over, and was relieved to find that the card was stamped and addressed. But the stamp looked very old-fashioned, and the postmark was so blurred that Lewis couldn't tell where the card had been mailed from. The card was addressed in a neat, curlicued hand.

Master Lewis Barnavelt
100 High Street
New Zebedee, Michigan

There was no return address.

Lewis stood there in the moonlight with the card in his hand. Maybe Rose Rita had gotten up in the middle of the night to play him a practical joke. Maybe—but it didn't seem likely. Lewis turned the card over and looked at the blank side again. His eyes opened wide. Now there was writing on the card.

Venio

Lewis's hand began to tremble. He had read about writing in invisible ink, but he had always heard that you had to dust the message with special powders or hold it over the fire to make the letters appear. This message had appeared all by itself.

And Lewis knew what the message said. He could read a little Latin, because he had been an altar boy once, and he knew what *Venio* meant: I come. Suddenly Lewis felt very afraid. He was afraid of being alone in the dark hallway. But as he stepped quickly across the hall to snap on the light, the card slipped out of his hand. It actually felt as if someone had grabbed it and pulled it away. Lewis panicked and flung himself at the wall switch. Warm yellow light flooded the hallway of the old house. There was no one there. But the card was gone.

CHAPTER THREE

The next morning, as soon as he got up, Lewis went downstairs to look for the mysterious postcard. He looked under the hall rug, and into the cracks between the floorboards. He looked into the blue Willoware vase where Jonathan kept his canes. He looked everywhere. The card had vanished. None of the cracks in the floor was wide enough for it to have slipped through, and the card couldn't very well have floated back out through the covered mail slot. *Where did it go?*

Lewis didn't feel like talking to Uncle Jonathan about the card, but as he ate his Cheerios that morning, a comfortable explanation occurred to him. The card was probably just part of Uncle Jonathan's magic.

Lewis had lived in the home of a practicing wizard for over a year now, and during that time he had come to expect strange sights and sounds. The mirror on the coat rack showed you your face when you looked in it— sometimes. But more often than not, it would show you Roman ruins in the desert or Mayan pyramids or Melrose Abbey in Scotland. There was an organ in the front parlor that sang radio commercials. And the stained-glass windows in the enormous old house changed their pictures from time to time, all by themselves. Maybe the ghostly card was one of Jonathan's little jokes. Lewis could have found out if his answer was right by asking Jonathan, since Jonathan controlled all the magic in the house. But he was afraid to ask. If his answer was wrong, he didn't want to know about it.

One afternoon in the middle of October, Lewis decided to go back to school early. Most of the time he waited out the noon hour at home, because he was afraid of getting beat up. But today he was going back early because Rose Rita had talked him into it.

Lewis and Rose Rita had had a long talk about his fears. She had tried to persuade him that the only way to conquer his fears was to meet them head-on. He had to force himself to go back to the playground right after lunch. After the first time, the second time would be easier, and so on. This was the way Rose Rita argued. Lewis had been stubborn at first, but he had finally agreed to try it her way. To make things easier for him,

Rose Rita had agreed to meet him in the alley next to the school. He wouldn't have to get into a football game or anything. The two of them would just stand around and talk. They could talk about the model Roman galley they were building out of balsa wood. It would be a lot of fun.

When Lewis got to the school, he peered down the long narrow alley. No Rose Rita. At the far end he could hear kids shouting and playing. Cautiously, he began to edge his way down the alley toward the playground. He always expected to get jumped, and sometimes it really happened.

Lewis had gotten about halfway down the alley when he heard something off to his left. It sounded like grunting and scuffling. Lewis turned and saw two kids fighting in the dark shadowy space between the buttresses of the Episcopal church. The kids were Rose Rita and Woody Mingo.

Lewis stood watching, paralyzed with fear. Woody had one hand around Rose Rita's waist, and with his other hand he was pulling her hair. Hard, so that it must really have hurt. But Rose Rita said nothing. Her eyes were closed, and her teeth were set in a rigid grimace.

"Come on," Woody snarled. "Take it back!"

"No."

"Take it *back*!"

"I said no, and—ow!—I meant—*no*!"

Woody grinned his nastiest grin. "Okay then—" He gave Rose Rita's hair a short vicious yank. Her grimace got tighter, and her teeth ground together. But she still refused to scream.

Lewis didn't know what to do. Should he run and get the principal, or go for the police? Or should he try to take on Woody all by himself? He thought about Woody's knife, and he was afraid.

Now Woody saw Lewis. He laughed, just the way he had when he stole Lewis's hat.

"Hey, fat guts! Arncha gonna rescue yer girl friend?" Woody gave Rose Rita's hair another yank, and she winced.

Rose Rita opened her eyes and glanced at Lewis. "Go away, Lewis!" she hissed. "Just go away!"

Lewis stood there, clenching and unclenching his fists. He looked toward the street, where cars were slowly rolling past. He looked toward the playground, where he could hear kids laughing and shouting and playing.

"C'mon, lard ass! You wanna try'n take me? Let's see ya try!"

Lewis turned and ran. Down the alley, out onto the sidewalk, across the intersection, up Green Street toward home. His feet slapped the pavement under him, and he could hear himself crying as he ran. He stopped halfway down Green Street because he couldn't run any more. His side hurt and his head ached and he wished that he were dead. When he had finally gotten his breath back, he wiped his eyes, blew his nose, and trotted the rest of the way home.

Uncle Jonathan was raking leaves in the front yard when Lewis came stomping moodily up the sidewalk.

"Hi, Lewis!" he called, waving cheerfully with his pipe. "Did they let school out early, or . . ."

Clang went the front gate. Slam went the front door a few seconds after. Jonathan dropped his rake and went in to see what was wrong.

He found Lewis crying with his head on the dining room table.

"God-dam dirty rotten no-good god-dam dirty . . ." was all Lewis would say, over and over.

Jonathan sat down in the chair next to him and put his arm around him. "Come on, Lewis," he said gently. "It's okay. What's wrong? Do you want to tell me what happened?"

Lewis wiped his eyes and blew his nose several times. Then, slowly and brokenly, he told his uncle the whole story. ". . . and I ran away and she'll never want to have anything to do with me ever again," he sobbed. "I wish I was *dead*!"

"Oh, I doubt if Rosie is going to scratch you off her social list," said Jonathan, smiling and patting him on the shoulder. "She just wanted to take care of herself, that's all. She's a real tomboy, and if she got into a fight with Woody, I guess she figured she could handle herself."

Lewis turned and looked at Jonathan through his tears. "You mean she won't hate me on account of I'm a coward and a weakling?"

"You're not either one of those," said Jonathan. "And anyway, if Rosie had wanted a lug for a best friend, she'd have found a lug. She's a very stubborn girl, and she does what she wants to do. And I think she likes you a lot."

"You do?"

"Mm-hmm. Now, I'm going to go finish raking the leaves, so we can have a bonfire in the driveway tonight. I'll write you a note Monday so you won't be in trouble with Miss Haggerty, and—well, why don't you go work on that ship model?"

Lewis smiled gratefully at his uncle. He hiccupped a few times, as he often did after he had been crying. "Okay, Uncle Jonathan. Thanks a lot."

Lewis went up to his room, and for the rest of the afternoon he was all wrapped up in the world of Greek and Roman triremes, and the great sea battles of Salamis and Actium. Just before dinner the phone rang. Lewis took the stairs two at a time, and almost fell on his face.

"Hi!" he panted as he picked up the receiver. "Is that you, Rose Rita?"

He heard a giggle at the other end. "If it hadn't of been, what would you have done?"

Lewis felt relieved. "Are you mad at me?" he asked.

"Unh-uh. I just called to find out what happened to you."

Lewis felt his face getting red. "I felt kinda sick so I went home. Did Woody beat you up?"

"Nope. A couple of the teachers came by and made us stop fighting. I would've fixed him if it hadn't've been for my darned hair. I think I'll get a crew cut."

"How come you were fighting?"

"Oh, I told him he was a dirty little sneak thief for stealing your hat, and he wanted me to take it back and I wouldn't."

Lewis was silent. He felt the way he had when Rose Rita had said that she wished she had been there to keep Woody from stealing the hat. It was a confusing feeling. He was grateful to her for sticking up for him, but it felt awful not to be able to fight and win your own battles. Boys were supposed to be able to do that.

"Are you okay?" Rose Rita asked. Lewis had been silent for a whole minute.

"Uh . . . yeah, sure. I was . . . I was just thinking," Lewis stammered. "Woody didn't hurt you, did he?"

Rose Rita snorted disdainfully. "Oh, he wouldn't do anything to me but pull my hair because I'm a *gurr-rul*. Hey, Lewis?"

"Yeah?"

"Let's get to work on that ship again. You want to bring it over to my house tonight?"

"Okay."

"See you after dinner. Bye."

"Bye."

Lewis was relieved to know that Rose Rita didn't hate him for running away. But he kept thinking about the fight between her and Woody, and that night he had a dream about it. In the dream, Woody had knocked Rose Rita down, and her head was bleeding. Lewis grabbed him and socked him and then Woody pulled his knife and held it up in front of Lewis's nose. Then Woody said, "I'm gonna cut your tongue out!" and Lewis awoke suddenly. He was sitting up in bed and his pajamas were drenched with sweat. It was a long time before he could get back to sleep again.

The next morning when Lewis got up, he decided that he was going to get thin and tough like Woody. He got down on the floor and tried to do ten pushups, but he could only do three before he collapsed. Then he tried sit-ups, but when he lay down flat on his back, he couldn't struggle up to a sitting position unless he thrashed around and used his elbows. He stood up and tried to touch his toes without bending his knees, but he couldn't do it. Trying made his head ache. Finally he tried jumping jacks. They were fun because you could clap your hands over your head when you did them. But the flab on Lewis's thighs clapped too, when his legs came together, and this sound depressed him. Also, he was afraid of bringing down the plaster in the room below. So he gave up and went downstairs to have breakfast.

It was Saturday morning, and Mrs. Zimmermann had come over to make breakfast. Although she lived next door, she usually cooked for the Barnavelts, and on Saturdays she always made something very special for breakfast. It might be doughnuts or pancakes and sausages or strawberry shortcake, or french toast with comb honey and peach preserves. This morning, Mrs. Zimmermann was making waffles. Lewis watched her as she poured some of the rich yellow batter onto the black iron grid. Then he remembered his resolution.

"Uh . . . Mrs. Zimmermann?" he said.

"Yes, Lewis?"

"I, uh, don't think I'll have any waffles this morning. Could I just have a bowl of corn flakes?"

Mrs. Zimmermann turned and looked at him strangely. She was about to go over and feel his forehead when she remembered what Jonathan had told her about the fight between Woody and Rose Rita. Mrs. Zimmermann was a very shrewd woman, and it didn't take her long to guess what Lewis had up his sleeve. So she shrugged her shoulders and said, "Okay. That'll just be a little more for me and your uncle."

Lewis managed to hold to his resolve all the way through breakfast. It was pure torture to see all those nice golden waffles and that thick maple syrup being passed back and forth in front of his nose. But he swallowed hard and ate his soggy, tasteless cornflakes.

After breakfast, Lewis went down to the junior high gym to work out. He punched the punching bag until his fists were sore. Then he rolled up his sleeve and flexed the muscle in his right arm. He couldn't tell if anything was happening, so he walked across the basketball court to find Mr. Hartwig. Mr. Hartwig was the gym instructor. He was a big cheerful man who was always throwing medicine balls at you and telling you to hit that line and suck in your gut and hup-two-three-four and stuff like that. When Lewis found him, Mr. Hartwig was organizing some informal boxing matches among boys who just seemed to be standing around doing nothing.

"Hi, Mr. Hartwig!" Lewis yelled. "Hey, can I see you for a minute?"

Mr. Hartwig smiled. "Sure thing, Lewis. What can I do for you?"

Lewis rolled up his sleeve again and held out his arm. He flexed the muscle, or what was supposed to be the muscle. "Do you see anything, Mr. Hartwig?" asked Lewis, hopefully.

Mr. Hartwig tried hard to keep from smiling. He knew Lewis, and he knew something about his problems. "Well, I see your arm," he said slowly. "Have you been working out today?"

"Yeah. Kinda. Doesn't it show?" Lewis flexed his arm again. He was getting embarrassed with all those kids standing around watching. Normally he wouldn't have done anything like this in front of them, but he really had to know. Mr. Hartwig was an expert. He could tell if Lewis's muscles were getting bigger.

Mr. Hartwig put his arm around Lewis and took him aside. "Listen, Lewis," he said quietly, "it takes more than five minutes with a punching bag to build up your muscles. You have to work at it for weeks and months and even years. So don't be discouraged if nothing happens right away. Okay? Now go back and hit that bag!" Mr. Hartwig smiled kindly and gave Lewis a light playful jab in the stomach, which was what he did when he liked you. Lewis winced. He thanked Mr. Hartwig and went back to the punching bag.

But his heart really wasn't in it now. If it was going to take years for him to build up a manly physique, he might as well knock it off and have lunch. It was almost one o'clock, and he was getting hungry.

Later, Lewis was sitting at the counter in Heemsoth's Drug Store. He had just had two hot dogs and two large cherry Cokes for lunch. Now he was leafing through a Captain Marvel comic book. Captain Marvel was slugging it out with the usual collection of crooks and villains. His uppercuts landed with sounds like ZOK! and POW! Lewis had tried a few uppercuts, but they had never landed on anybody's chin. The kids he had tried to use them on had just stepped away and laughed.

Lewis read all the stories in the comic book and then

flipped to the back. There were ads there for things like a Vacutex, an evil-looking gadget that resembled a hypodermic. It was supposed to suck out unsightly blackheads. That was more of a teenager's problem. Lewis had other things to worry about.

He turned to the last page, and there was the Charles Atlas ad. It was always there, and it was always the same. There was a little cartoon story about a 97-pound weakling who got strong so he could get even with the guy who kicked sand in his face at the beach. And there at the bottom of the ad was Charles Atlas himself, in a white bathing suit that always made Lewis think of a baby's diaper. Mr. Atlas looked as if he were covered with grease, and he was bulging and rippling all over with muscles. He was shaking his fist at Lewis and daring him to try his Dynamic Tension Exercises. Under the picture of Mr. Atlas was the little coupon that you were supposed to cut out. Lewis had been on the point of cutting it out many times, but he had always stopped for some reason or other. Now, he ripped out the page, folded it neatly, and slipped it into his pocket. That afternoon when he got home, he put the coupon in an envelope with a quarter and mailed it off to Charles Atlas.

Lewis kept at his diet and his pushups for three or four days, but by the end of that time it was getting pretty boring. He kept feeling his arms, but it didn't seem to him that any new muscles were arriving. And dieting meant that he felt crabby a good deal of the time. He began to realize that Mr. Hartwig was right. Getting thin and tough like Woody took work. You had to deny yourself things that you really wanted, and you had to slave away at things that were really very dull, like exercises. And even then, you couldn't be absolutely positively sure that you would get what you wanted after all your hard work.

Lewis began to weaken, and then he gave in completely. He decided that he would take a break and go back to his plan when he felt better. Before long he was munching Reese's Peanut Butter Cups and taking second helpings of strawberry shortcake with whipped cream. He stopped doing pushups and he never went near the punching bag again. Now and then he would check the mail to see if the Charles Atlas booklet had arrived, but it was never there.

If only there was an easy way of getting to be strong! Lewis thought about Grampa Barnavelt's lucky piece. Wouldn't it be great if it really was magic? Magic in a way that would let him mow down his enemies and protect Rose Rita from harm? That would sure be something! Then he could forget about dieting and pushups. Then . . .

But every time Lewis had this daydream, he remembered that Mrs. Zimmermann had examined the coin, and she had flatly stated that it was not magic. Mrs. Zimmermann was an expert on magic. She ought to know.

On the other hand, experts had been wrong before, like those people who claimed that men would never be able to fly. Lewis would argue with himself this way, back and forth, pro and con, until he was sick of the whole business. Then he would go up to his room and take the coin out of his drawer and press it between his thumb and index finger. Wasn't there a tingle there? No, there wasn't. Then he would get angry and shove the coin back in the drawer and slam the drawer shut. He did this over and over again, but nothing ever happened. Lewis fiddled with the coin so much, wishing over it and pressing it, that he began to think of it as his "magic coin." The phrase "magic coin" kept running through his mind like a broken record. He tried to think of other things, but the phrase kept coming back. Magic coin. Magic coin. Was it just wishful thinking, or was there something else at work?

CHAPTER FOUR

On a bright sunny Saturday afternoon in late October, Lewis and Rose Rita were poking around in Jonathan's library. Some people put a bookcase in a room and call the room a library, but that was not Jonathan's way. His library was crammed, floor to ceiling, with books. Lewis often went to this room to browse or just to sit and think. Today he was there with Rose Rita, looking for a Latin motto to put on the sail of the Roman galley they were building. The galley had turned into quite a project. Lewis and Rose Rita had sat up late many nights with strips of balsa wood and rubber cement and model airplane glue. They had the ship about half finished, but, as often happens, they had gotten hung up on an unimportant detail. Lewis had drawn a picture of Duilius, the great Roman admiral, on the sail, and he had found a motto to go with the picture: IN HOC SIGNO VINCES. The motto came from a carton of Pall Mall cigarettes; it wasn't appropriate, but it was the only one Lewis could find. Rose Rita had informed him that she thought the motto was stupid and senseless. Now the two of them were digging through the Latin books in Jonathan's collection, looking for a reasonable, appropriate, and suitably dignified motto. In other words, they were looking for a motto that Rose Rita liked.

"You know, Lewis, it would kind of help if your uncle would keep his books in better order," Rose Rita complained.

"It would, huh? Okay, what's wrong with the way my uncle keeps his books?" Lewis was getting tired of Rose Rita's crabbing, and he was beginning to fight back.

"What's wrong? Oh, not much. Just look at them! This section here is supposed to be Latin books, and there's adventure novels, and old phone books, and even a book by Mrs. Zimmermann."

Lewis was startled. He didn't know that Mrs. Zimmermann had written a book. "Gee, that's weird. What kind of a book is it?"

"I dunno. Let's see." Rose Rita took down from the bookshelf a dusty book in a black leather pebble-grained cover. A title was stamped on the spine in gold letters. It said:

by
F. H. Zimmermann
D. Mag.A.

Rose Rita and Lewis knelt down on the floor to examine the book. The first page was the title page. It said:

A FREE INQUIRY INTO
THE PROPERTIES OF MAGIC AMULETS

A dissertation submitted to
the Faculty of Magic Arts of the University of
Göttingen, in partial fulfillment of the
requirements for the Degree of
DOCTOR MAGICORUM ARTIUM
(Doctor of Magic Arts)

by
Florence Helene Zimmermann
June 13, 1922

English Language Copy

Lewis was amazed. Amazed, and fascinated. He knew
that Mrs. Zimmermann had gone to college to learn how
to be a witch, but he didn't know about this book.

"I bet your uncle would be mad if he knew we were
looking at this," said Rose Rita, giggling.

Lewis glanced nervously toward the door. At one time Jonathan had kept his magic books out on the shelves with all the other books in his collection. But he had gotten concerned about Lewis's interest in magic, and so one day he had scooped up all the magic books he could find and carried them off to his bedroom closet. That was where they were now, locked up. All but this one, which Jonathan had forgotten about.

"Yeah, I'll bet he doesn't even know it's here," said Lewis.

"Well, serves him right for keeping such a messy library," said Rose Rita. "Come on, let's see what's in it."

Lewis and Rose Rita sat down on the floor and began leafing through Mrs. Zimmermann's book. They found out quite a bit about magic amulets. They read about the strange parchment found on the body of Bishop Anselm of Würzburg, and the lost amulet of Queen Catherine de Medici of France. Finally, at the end of the book, they came to a chapter with this title:

ON THE VARIOUS METHODS
OF TESTING AMULETS

Lewis thought about the coin in his drawer upstairs, and he began to get very interested. But what he read at first was disappointing. The book just said what Mrs. Zimmermann had said the night they found the coin: only a real wizard could test an amulet. Mrs. Zimmermann had tested the three-cent piece, using the method recommended by her own book. And the coin had turned out to be just a coin.

Rose Rita was getting pretty bored with amulets. "Come on, Lewis," she said impatiently. "We're wasting a lot of time. Let's go see if we can find something nice to put on our ship." She closed the book and started to get up.

"Wait a minute," said Lewis, opening the book again. "There's one more page. Let's see what's on it." Rose Rita heaved a deep sigh and sat down again.

They turned to the last page, and this is what they read:

There are a few extremely powerful amulets that will not respond to the tests I have described. These amulets are very rare. I have never handled such an amulet, nor have I ever seen one, but it is said that one was owned by King Solomon, and that Simon Magus somehow contrived to steal one, so that for a time he seemed to be a very great magician indeed.

These amulets of which I speak are so powerful that they do not appear to be magic at all. They do not respond to any of the standard tests. Yet, I am told that they will respond to this test:

Place the amulet in your left hand, cross yourself three times, and say the following prayer:

Immo haud daemonorum, umquam et numquam, urbi et orbi, quamquam Azazel magnopere Thoth et Urim et Thummim in nomine Tetragrammaton. Fiat, fiat. Amen.

Then, if the amulet is truly one of those I have described above, it will produce a tingling sensation in the hand. The tingling will last for only a few seconds, and after that the amulet will seem as dull and dead as any ordinary object. It will seem dead, but it will not be dead. I may add here . . .

Lewis looked up from the book. There was a strange light in his eyes.

"Hey!" he said. "Why don't we go up and get Grampa Barnavelt's coin and see if it's one of these?"

Rose Rita gave him an exasperated look. "Oh, come on, Lewis! She tested it for you the night we found it. Remember?"

"Yeah, but she didn't use this test. It says right here that the really strong amulets don't respond to the test she used."

"Unh-huh. And it also says that these strong amulets are very rare."

"Well, Grampa's coin *might* be one of them. You can never tell."

Rose Rita slammed the book shut and stood up. "Oh, all *right!* Go get your dumb coin and bring it down here and say dumb magic words over it and we'll see what happens. I'm so sick of this whole business that I'd like to drop your stupid coin down the sewer. Now, if you say all this junk here and nothing happens, will you shut up?"

"Yeah," said Lewis, grinning.

Lewis ran upstairs and yanked open the drawer of his bedside table. After a bit of fumbling and poking around, he found the coin. He could hear his heart beating and his face felt flushed. When he got back to the library, Rose Rita was sitting there in the leather armchair. She was leafing through a big book full of pictures of sailing ships.

"Well?" she said, without looking up. "Did you find it?"

Lewis gave her a dirty look. He wanted her to be interested in what he was doing. "Yeah, I found it. Now, come on and help me."

"Why do you need my help? You can read, can't you?"

"Yeah, I can read, but I don't have three hands. You have to hold the book for me so I can read it while I make the sign of the Cross with one hand and hold the coin with the other hand."

"Oh, all right."

There was a set of double doors in the middle of one wall of the library. They were glass doors, and they opened right out onto the side yard of the house. Lewis and Rose Rita took up their positions in front of these doors. Lewis stood with his back to the doors. The light fell over his shoulder onto the pages of the book that Rose Rita held up before him. In his left hand, Lewis held the coin. With his right hand, he slowly made the sign of the Cross on himself. He did it three times. Then he began to chant, the way he had heard Father Cahalen do during Mass:

"Immo haud daemonorum, umquam et numquam . . ."

As Lewis chanted, the room began to get darker. The light faded from the bright orange leaves of the maple tree outside, and now a strong wind was rattling the glass doors. Suddenly the doors flew open, and the wind got into the room. It riffled madly through the dictionary on the library table, scattered papers across the floor, and knocked all the lampshades galley-west. Lewis turned. He stood there silent, staring out into the strange twilight. His hand was still clenched tight around the coin.

Rose Rita closed the book and glanced nervously at Lewis. From where she stood she could not see his face. "Gee, that was weird," she said. "I mean, it was just like . . . like as if you had made it get dark outside."

"Yeah," said Lewis. "It was funny how it happened." He did not move an inch, but just stood there, looking out at the night.

"Did . . . did anything happen to the coin?" Rose Rita's voice was tense and frightened-sounding.

"Nope."

"You sure?"

"Yeah, I'm sure. It's just a dud. C'mon, let's get back to work."

Lewis moved quickly to the glass doors and shut them. Then he helped Rose Rita pick up the things that the little hurricane had strewn about the room. As he went back and forth, straightening and arranging things, he was careful to keep his face turned away from Rose Rita. The coin had jumped in his hand, and he did not want her to know.

CHAPTER FIVE

As soon as Rose Rita had gone home, Lewis clattered down the cellar stairs to his uncle's workshop. He dug around in the tool box until he found the wire clippers, and, after a little struggling, managed to cut the little metal loop that held the coin to the watch chain. Then he ran upstairs and rooted around in the drawer of his bedside table until he found his old St. Anthony medal. He had been given the medal after his first Holy Communion, and he had worn it for a while, but then he had gotten tired of it. After a lot of fussing with wire clippers and pliers, he managed to get the coin hooked onto the chain, where the St. Anthony medal had been before. He fastened the chain around his neck and went to the mirror to look at himself.

October turned into November, and the weather got colder. Lewis could see his breath in the morning when he opened the front door. He wore the magic coin all the time now: to church, to school, and even in bed at night. Jonathan, Mrs. Zimmermann, and Rose Rita had all at different times seen the chain around his neck, but they had assumed he was just wearing his St. Anthony medal again. Whenever he was undressing in his room, Lewis made sure that the door was shut and locked.

It would have been hard for Lewis to explain how the coin made him feel. The closest thing he could compare it to was the feeling he got when he went to the Bijou Theatre and saw a pirate movie. Lewis loved the cutlass duels and thundering broadsides and smoke and battles and blood. When he stepped out onto the street after seeing one, he could almost feel the sword hanging at his side and the long pirate pistol stuck in his belt. As he walked home, he imagined that he was wrapped in a heavy cloak and stalking toward the docks in some Spanish port, or pacing moodily on his quarter-deck as the planks under him shook to cannonade after cannonade. He felt grim and strong and brave and heartless and cruel. It was a good feeling, and it usually lasted about half of the way home. Then he was just plain old Lewis again.

The feeling that the magic coin gave Lewis was a bit like the pirate-movie feeling, except that the coin feeling lasted longer. The coin did other things for him too: for one thing, he found that his head was full of schemes and plots. He would walk along dreaming up ways to get even with Woody Mingo and the other kids who bothered him. Of course, he had dreamed of revenge before the magic coin came into his life, but his planning had never been so good. Sometimes Lewis had to shake his head to get rid of a plan that was too awful to think about.

And it seemed to Lewis that he was dreaming a lot more at night now. The dreams seemed to be in color, with music playing in the background—stirring military music. Lewis would dream that he was riding at the head of an army or leading his knights up over the walls of a castle. There were other dreams too, really frightening ones, but he could never remember them. He just woke up with the feeling that he had had them.

So Lewis wore the coin and waited for it to do something for him. And around about this time Woody Mingo began to make life really miserable for Lewis.

It was as if Woody sat up nights thinking of mean things to do: he managed to get a seat near Lewis in school, and when Miss Haggerty's back was turned, he would dart across the aisle and pinch Lewis in the neck. Hard, so that it hurt for a long time afterwards. Or he would goose Lewis when they were in the bathroom together, or he would put dead mice in Lewis's briefcase because he knew that Lewis was very much afraid of dead animals. Probably the most maddening thing that Woody did was to march Lewis down the stairs of the

school during fire drills. Lewis's school was a tall old brick building with shaky wooden staircases. The sixth-grade room was on the second floor, and when the fire bell rang and everyone lined up at the top of the stair-case, Woody would slip in behind Lewis. Then he would put one hand in each of Lewis's hip pockets and march him down the stairs, saying, "Right butt, left butt, hup-two-three-four, *march!*" until Lewis got to the bottom, shaken and sick and almost in tears.

Lewis didn't understand why Woody had decided to pick on him. It was like those kids who jumped out at you when you were walking down the street, and wouldn't let you by till you had told them your name, and they had pounded you a couple of times on the arm. They were bullies, and so was Woody. Kids like that always seemed to be attracted to Lewis. He had hoped that his magic coin would help him to stand up to Woody but so far it hadn't. Lewis might be walking down the street with the coin around his neck, imagi-ning that he was Blackbeard the pirate or Tom Corbett, Space Cadet. Then he would run into Woody and all his courage would evaporate, and he would find himself thinking about the red-handled jacknife that Woody carried in his pocket. But maybe the coin would help him yet. He hoped that it would.

One night Lewis went to bed thinking about how to get even with Woody Mingo. He fell asleep amid day-dreams of exploding baseballs and poisoned peanut butter sandwiches, and trap doors that dropped people into cauldrons of boiling oil. So perhaps it is not very surprising that he had a wild and exciting dream that night.

In the dream Lewis had become a tall, big-boned Viking chieftain. He and his companions were fighting off an attack by some Indians. Lewis recognized the place where they were fighting. It was Wilder Creek Park, which was just outside the city limits. Lewis had been there on picnics a number of times. In the dream the wooden tables and the brick cook-stoves had vanished, and the park was weedy and overgrown. He and his men were drawn into a ring in the middle of the park, and Indians were attacking them from all sides.

The dream seemed to go on for hours. Knives whizzed past and arrows flew. Lewis was wielding a heavy battle ax, and each time he swung it, an enemy fell. He waded into the throng of painted savages, laying about him mightily and urging his companions on with deep-throated war cries. Lewis swung and swung, and Indians fell right and left, but still they kept on coming.

When he woke up the next morning, Lewis felt exhausted. Exhausted, but glowing and triumphant, as if he had just made an eighty-yard touchdown run on a football field. He sat there on the edge of his bed for a while, thinking about the dream. Suddenly he reached in under his pajama top and touched the coin. Darn! It felt perfectly ordinary, just as it always had, except for the time it had jumped and tingled during the saying of the magic spell from Mrs. Zimmermann's book. Lewis felt disappointed. He knew that very powerful amulets were supposed to seem dead, but just the same, he was disappointed. After a dream like that, the coin ought to have felt red-hot. At least, that's what Lewis thought.

He picked the coin up and eyed it skeptically. It hadn't really done anything for him yet. Nothing real, that is, except give him strange feelings and dreams. And maybe the coin hadn't even done that. Maybe the feelings and dreams had just come out of his own mind.

Lewis felt confused. He thought about the coin some more as he was getting dressed. It certainly was true that the coin had jumped in his hand that once—or had it? Lewis knew that you could get some very funny pinches and twinges in your body. Once on a hot summer day he had had the feeling that a worm was crawling across his back. But when he took off his shirt and looked, there was nothing there. What if . . . oh, the heck with it! Phooey on it! Lewis shook his head to get rid of all the conflicting thoughts that were banging around in his skull. By the time he had finished dressing, he felt better. In fact, he was beginning to get that pirate-movie feeling again. Lewis looked at himself in the mirror. He patted the coin. Maybe the coin had heard him. Maybe it knew that he was having doubts about its powers. Maybe it just wanted a chance to prove itself. Okay. He would give it a chance. Today would be the day the coin helped him take care of Woody Mingo.

CHAPTER SIX

That morning at breakfast, Lewis asked Mrs. Zimmermann to pack a lunch for him. He said that he was going to stay down at school during the noon hour. Jonathan and Mrs. Zimmermann both smiled happily. They were glad that Lewis was going to have fun with the other boys instead of skulking at home like a fugitive. And when Lewis went out the door, they saw that he was grinning from ear to ear.

"Rose Rita has been a good influence on him," said Jonathan, as he poured himself a second cup of coffee. "I hope she keeps it up."

Mrs. Zimmermann stood there staring at the front door. She scratched her chin thoughtfully. "Maybe it's good," she said, slowly, "but I can't help feeling that there's something funny about Lewis these days. I can't quite put my finger on it, but there's something wrong. Did you notice how tired he looked? Around the eyes, I mean. And yet he was raring to go. It's odd."

Jonathan shrugged. "It's always odd when a boy like Lewis does something different. But I wouldn't worry about him. I think he knows what he's doing."

Lewis hummed marching songs all the way to school. He really felt great. But when noontime came and he had eaten his lunch, he felt different. He began to get worried. By the time he had reached the edge of the playground, he could feel his courage ebbing away. Should he turn around and go home? Lewis paused. Then he pulled himself together, patted the amulet, and walked forward in quick nervous strides.

It was a gray November day on the playground. The football and baseball fields were covered with frozen footprints and bicycle ruts. Puddles of ice lay here and there. Lewis saw a group of boys getting ready to play football. They were lining up to be chosen, and the two captains were flipping a coin to see who got first choice. As Lewis drew near, he saw that one of the boys in the group was Woody. And once again Lewis's courage failed. He felt like going home. But he fought down his fear, and stayed.

Lewis slipped into the group of boys that were waiting to be chosen. He stood there with his hands in his pockets, hoping that no one would notice him. Near him, a boy who had been jumping up and down and slapping his sides stopped jumping and stared at Lewis as if he were a visitor from outer space. What was old lardo doing here?

One by one the boys got picked, until only two were left unchosen. They were Woody and Lewis. Woody glanced over at Lewis and grinned.

"Well, if it ain't lard ass. Djer uncle letcha out of yer cage today?"

Lewis stared hard at the ground.

The two captains were Tom Lutz and Dave Shellenberger. It was Tom's turn to choose, and he glanced from Woody to Lewis. Woody was good at sports, but the boys avoided choosing him because he was such a troublemaker.

"Oh, well. C'mon, Woody," Tom grumbled. Woody walked over to the group of boys on Tom's side.

For a minute it looked as if Dave Shellenberger would tell Lewis to go home. That was what usually happened on the rare occasions when Lewis showed up to play games with the other boys. But this time, for some reason, Dave chose Lewis. He motioned for him to come over to his side.

"C'mon, fatty," he said. "We'll make you our center. Need some beef in the line."

Lewis was in the game. He could hardly believe it.

After the kickoff, Lewis's side wound up with the ball. Lewis stood there, bent over, legs wide apart, rubbing the football back and forth over the frozen ground. The quarterback started a long count.

"Forty-three . . . twenty-four . . . three . . . zero . . . fourteen . . ."

Suddenly Lewis felt a sickening shock. He had been staring at the ground, and now he was on his back, looking up at the heavy gray sky.

"Ooops. Sorry. Guess I jumped the gun." It was Woody, of course.

"Hey, Woody, come on!" yelled Dave. "Cut out that kind of crap, will you?"

"I think lard ass here was off sides," said Woody, pointing down at Lewis.

"I was not, and stop callin' me lard ass!" Lewis was on his feet now, red-faced and angry.

"That's your name, lard ass," said Woody, carelessly. "Got any other names?"

Lewis hauled off and punched Woody in the stomach. Woody clutched at his middle. Pain and surprise were in his eyes. The punch had really hurt.

Several boys who were standing around gasped. Somebody yelled, "Fight! Fight!" and a circle formed around the two boys. Woody was angry now. He spat on the ground and swore. "Okay, you tub of guts," he snarled, moving in with his fists up. "Now you're gonna get it."

Lewis backed away. He felt like turning and running.

But now Woody was on him, swinging hard. The blows fell on Lewis's shoulders in a stinging rain. Lewis lunged and got his arms around Woody. Now the two of them were rolling over and over on the ground. Woody came out on top, and Lewis felt his head being pushed down into a frozen puddle. The thin ice cracked, and cold water bit into Lewis's scalp.

Lewis looked up at the ring of expectant faces hovering against the sky. Woody was astride him, sneering and triumphant.

"Go ahead, lard ass. Tell 'em what your name is." Woody put his hand on Lewis's face and shoved. Icy water stung Lewis's ears.

"No."

"Go *on*, I said! Tell 'em your *name!*" Woody dug his knees into Lewis's sides. It was like being caught in a nutcracker.

Suddenly Lewis lurched upward, and Woody fell over on his back. Now they were rolling over and over again, and this time Lewis came up on top. He was sitting with his full weight on Woody's chest. But Woody had a free arm. He reached up and punched Lewis on the ear. It stung, but Lewis didn't move. He grabbed Woody by the hair and banged his head on the ground.

"Come on, Woody. Say you give up!"

Woody glared defiantly up at Lewis. "No."

Lewis raised his fist, but then he hesitated. He had always been told that it was bad to hit someone who was down. Maybe he could just sit on Woody till Woody gave in. But as he was thinking this, some other power seized Lewis's hand and brought it down hard on Woody's nose. Blood gushed from Woody's nostrils. It ran down over his mouth and chin.

Lewis jerked his hand back and clutched it to his chest, as if he was afraid of what it might do if he let it loose again. When he looked down, he saw that Woody was staring up at him, his eyes wide with fear.

"I . . . I give up," Woody stammered.

Lewis got up and backed away. The boys who had been watching the fight looked from one to another in disbelief. No one knew what to say. They had all figured that Woody would wipe up the earth with Lewis.

Woody got up slowly. He was crying and wiping his bloody nose with his sleeve. One boy ran into the school to get a cold cloth to hold to Woody's nose, while others were advising him to hold his head back and press the bridge of his nose with two fingers. For the time being, Lewis was a hero. Dave Shellenberger slapped him on the back and said, "Way to go, baby!" Another boy asked him if he'd been doing exercises. Finally, when Woody's nose had been taken care of, the boys asked Lewis if he'd like to play football with them some more. Dave said that he could be fullback if he wanted to. But Lewis said, "Gee, no thanks, fellas. I just remembered something I was supposed to do. I'll see you all later." He waved and walked away.

Lewis didn't really have anything that he had to do. He just wanted to be alone with his thoughts. So he wandered off to a quiet part of the playground and started pacing. And as he paced, he thought.

He had figured that he would feel great after his victory, but he didn't. Strangely enough, he felt sorry for Woody, who had been showed up in front of all those kids. Woody had had a reputation as a tough guy. Now everybody would start picking on him. And something else was bothering Lewis. He hadn't intended to punch Woody in the nose. It was as if someone had grabbed his arm and brought it smashing down. Lewis knew that the amulet had done it, but all the same, he didn't like it. He didn't like the idea of being jerked around like a puppet on a string. He had wanted magic help, but he had wanted the help to stay under his control.

After he had paced a little more, Lewis pulled out his watch and looked at it. Lunch period was almost over. Maybe he would feel better if he told Rose Rita about what he had done—leaving out the part about the amulet, of course. Sure. That was a good idea. He would tell her all about his big fight with Woody, and she would be proud of him. And that would make him feel better about the whole business.

Lewis knew where he would find Rose Rita. She would be pitching in the girls' softball game. It was the wrong season for softball, but the girls weren't allowed to scrimmage around and get their skirts dirty in games like football, so they played softball all through the autumn until snow flew.

Lewis arrived at the girls' softball diamond just as Rose Rita was firing the ball up to the plate. The batter, a girl with yellow braids, swung like somebody chopping wood. She missed.

That was the end of the inning, and anyway the bell was ringing for the kids to come back to school. As Rose Rita walked off the field, Lewis noticed that she had a disgusted look on her face. But as soon as she saw him, she brightened up.

"Hi, Lewis!" she called, waving. She stopped in front of him, made a hideous face, and put her finger up to her forehead like a gun that was going to blow her brains out. "Yaah!" she said.

"What's wrong?" asked Lewis.

"Oh nothing. It's just that Lois Carver is such a rotten batter. I strike her out every time she comes up to bat. This last time I pitched to her with my eyes shut, just to see what would happen. But she struck out anyway."

"She did?" Lewis was only half listening to what Rose Rita was saying. He wanted to tell her all about the big fight.

"I got in a fight with Woody Mingo," he said.

Rose Rita looked surprised. "You did. Is that where you got that thick ear?"

"Yeah, but I gave him something worse. Pow! Right

in the kisser!" Lewis tried to imitate the punch he had used.

Rose Rita glanced at him skeptically. "Oh, come on, Lewis! Stop telling stories! You don't have to lie to *me*. I won't make fun of you because you got beat up."

Suddenly Lewis became very angry. He turned on Rose Rita and yelled at the top of his voice, "Okay, if *that's* the way you feel, I'll get somebody *else* to be my best friend!" He turned on his heel and stalked away, adding, over his shoulder, "See ya round!"

Lewis marched off toward the school building. He walked fast and didn't look back. By the time he got to the door, he found that he was crying.

CHAPTER SEVEN

As soon as Lewis got home from school that day, he called up Rose Rita, but her mother answered and said that she wasn't back yet. Later that evening, Lewis tried again, and got her. Both of them tried to apologize at once. Rose Rita had heard from several people about Lewis's fight with Woody, and she said that she was sorry for having doubted him. Lewis said he was sorry he had lost his temper. By the time the conversation was over with, everything seemed to be all right again. At least, for the time being.

A few days after his fight with Woody Mingo, Lewis began to get the feeling that company was coming. He didn't know why he had this feeling, but he did have it.

It started when he was setting the table. He dropped a knife, and then he remembered the old saying: If you drop a knife, then company is coming. Normally Lewis didn't believe in old sayings and superstitions. But the feeling he got was so strong that he began to wonder if there wasn't something in the old proverb after all.

That night, Lewis sat on his cushioned window seat and watched the snow come down. It was the first snowfall of the winter. Lewis was always very impatient for the first snow, and if it didn't stay on the ground, he got angry. But tonight's snow looked as if it was going to stay. It swirled past his window and drifted into dreamy shapes under the tall chestnut tree. It sparkled in the cold light of the street lamp across from Lewis's house. It piled up on window ledges and doorsteps.

Lewis sat there thinking about all the things he would do when there was a lot of snow on the ground. Like sledding down Murray's Hill with Rose Rita. Like walking home from church at night with Jonathan and Mrs. Zimmermann. Like wandering the snowy streets alone by moonlight and imagining that the snow-wall between the sidewalk and the street was the wall of a castle, and that he was pacing the ramparts, planning how to hurl back an enemy assault.

Lewis closed his eyes. He felt very happy. Then a picture appeared before his closed eyes. A very strange picture.

Lewis often saw pictures in the dark, just before he

went to sleep at night. Sometimes he would see, quite clearly, the streets of Constantinople or London. He had never been to these cities, so he really didn't know what they looked like, but he imagined that he was looking at Constantinople or London. He saw domes and minarets and steeples and streets and avenues. They appeared in the darkness behind his eyelids.

The picture that came to Lewis now was the picture of a man walking up the Homer Road toward New Zebedee. The Homer Road was a winding country road that ran between New Zebedee and the very small town of Homer. Lewis had been over the Homer Road quite a few times this last summer, going to and from Mrs. Zimmermann's cottage on Lyon Lake. As Lewis watched, the picture moved. The man was walking straight up the center of the road, leaving footprints in the snow behind him. Since the only light in the picture was moonlight, Lewis could not see too much of the man. In fact, he could not see enough to tell whether the figure was a man or a woman—but somehow he felt sure it was a man. The man had a long coat on—it flapped around his ankles as he walked. And he was walking fast.

Now the man was passing the gas station at Eldridge Corners. He paused to look at the old rusty signpost, and then he took the fork that led past the humming, brightly lit power house. Now he was crossing the railroad tracks just outside the city limits.

Lewis opened his eyes and looked out into the snowy yard. He shook his head. He wasn't at all sure he liked the picture that had come before his eyes. He couldn't say why the dark figure frightened him, but it did. He hoped that it was not the company that was supposed to be coming.

One afternoon, not long after Lewis had had this strange nighttime vision, something else happened. Lewis was on his way home from Rose Rita's house. He was just walking along, staring at his shadow, when he noticed a piece of paper lying on the sidewalk in front of him. For some reason, he stopped and picked it up.

It was just a sheet of blue-ruled notebook paper that some kid had been practicing his handwriting on. At the top of the page was one of these double rainbows you had to make when you were warming up during handwriting class. And below that was a neat row of small v's, and another row, this one of capital V's. The capital V's all looked just like the V in *Venio*, the word that had appeared on the postcard.

Lewis could feel his heart beating. He glanced quickly down the page and saw the word he dreaded. It was written on the bottom line of the sheet.

Venio

Lewis felt sick and shivery. The word on the paper squirmed before his eyes. As Lewis stood there trembling, a sudden gust of wind snatched the paper from his hand and blew it across the street. He started to go after it, but the wind was blowing so hard that by the time he had run across to get it, the paper was gone. Gone like the postcard.

Lewis felt that sick chill again. His heart continued to beat in thick heavy beats under his winter coat. "*Venio* means 'I come,'" Lewis repeated to himself. "*Venio* means 'I come.'" But who was coming? The man Lewis had seen in his daydream? The dark figure on the Homer Road? Whoever it was, Lewis didn't want to meet him.

As he walked home, Lewis began to argue with himself. He always did this when he was trying to fight his fears down. He dreamed up "logical explanations" for the things he was afraid of, and sometimes these explanations made the fears go away—for a while, at any rate. By the time he got to his house, Lewis had persuaded himself that the midnight postcard was just something he had dreamed about. You couldn't always tell when you were sleeping and when you were awake, after all. He had just dreamed that he had gone downstairs and found a postcard with *Venio* written on it. But what about the paper he had just found on the street? Well (Lewis argued) that was just some show-offy grade-school kid who had learned to write Latin. That was all it was. It was just a coincidence that the kid had used the same word that appeared on the postcard. Or maybe Lewis had just imagined that he saw the word *Venio* on the piece of paper. It could have been Veronica, or some name like that . . .

As he hung up his coat and went in to have supper, Lewis went on arguing inside his head. He wasn't really convinced by his clever explanations, but they made him feel better. They helped him to fight off the black shapeless fear that was forming in his mind.

That evening Lewis decided to do his homework down at the public library. The library was a pleasant place to work, with its old scarred tables and green-shaded lamps. Lewis went there a lot, to browse or to look things up. He packed his books into his briefcase and stomped off toward the library through the snow, whistling cheerfully.

Lewis worked at the library till closing time, which was nine. Then he packed up his books again and got ready to leave. Nine was a little late for him to be walking the streets of New Zebedee alone, but he wasn't worried. Nothing bad ever happened in New Zebedee. And besides, he had his amulet with him.

Lewis was about three blocks from the library when he saw someone standing under the street lamp on the corner. At first he was scared. The dark figure on the Homer Road flashed before his eyes. But then he laughed. Why was he so silly? It was probably just old Joe DiMaggio.

There was a bum in New Zebedee who called himself Joe DiMaggio. He wore a New York Yankees baseball cap and handed out pens shaped like baseball bats. The pens were all inscribed "Joe DiMaggio." Sometimes Joe helped the police check the doors of the shops on Main Street. And sometimes he waited under street lamps to jump out at kids and yell "Boo!" at them. That was probably who it was standing there under the light. Good old Joe.

"Hi, there, Joe!" Lewis called, waving at the still figure.

The figure walked forward out of the circle of lamplight. Now it was standing before Lewis. Lewis smelled something. He smelled cold ashes. Cold wet ashes.

The tall muffled figure stood there, silent, towering over Lewis. Lewis felt queasy inside. Joe was just a short little guy. It couldn't be him standing there. Frantically, Lewis fumbled with the zipper on his coat. His hand closed over the part of his shirt where the amulet was, bunching up the cloth so that the hard little object was inside his fist. And at that the figure took one sudden gliding step forward and spread its arms wide.

Lewis let go of the amulet with a shriek. He turned and ran, ran for his life, stumbling over snowbanks and in and out of slush puddles and over slippery smooth patches of ice till he reached the stone steps of the library. Then he scrambled up the steps and banged violently with his hands on the glass doors. He banged till the palms of his hands stung. Nobody came.

At last he saw a light come on in the foyer of the library. Miss Geer was still there. Thank God.

Lewis stood there with his face and hands pressed against the glass. He was half out of his mind with fear. At any second he expected to feel hands clawing at his back, to be spun around and pressed into the face of—he didn't dare think what.

Finally Miss Geer came. She was an old lady and had arthritis, so she walked slowly. Now she was fumbling with the lock. Now the door swung inward.

"My goodness, Lewis, if I was to tell your uncle that you were pounding away to beat the band like that—" Miss Geer stopped her scolding when Lewis threw his arms around her and shook her frail old body with his frightened sobs.

"There, there, Lewis. It's all right, it's all right, what in the world . . ." Miss Geer was not a mean old lady by any means. She liked children, and she especially liked Lewis.

"For heaven's sake, Lewis, whatever has happened to make you—"

"Please, Miss Geer, call my uncle," Lewis sobbed. "Call him and tell him to come down and get me. There's somebody out there, and I'm scared!"

Miss Geer looked at him, and then she smiled kindly. She knew about children and their wild imaginations. "There, there, Lewis. Everything's all right. Just sit down here on the step and I'll go call your uncle. It'll only take a minute."

"No, don't go away, Miss Geer. Please don't. I . . . I want to come with you."

So Lewis followed Miss Geer into her office and stood shifting nervously from one foot to the other as she asked the operator to give her the Barnavelt residence. It seemed to Lewis that Jonathan was taking forever to get to the phone, but finally he answered. Then he and Miss Geer talked for a little while. Lewis couldn't tell much from the noises Miss Geer made, but it seemed obvious that Jonathan was puzzled. As well he might be.

A few minutes later, Jonathan's big black car pulled up in front of the library. Lewis and Miss Geer were waiting on the front steps. As soon as Lewis was in the car, Jonathan turned to him and said, "What happened?"

"It was . . . it was something pretty awful, Uncle Jonathan. It was a ghost or a monster or something, and it . . . it tried to get me." Lewis put his face in his hands and started to cry.

Jonathan put his arm around Lewis and tried to comfort him. "There, there, Lewis . . . don't cry. Everything's all right. It was probably just somebody trying to scare you. Halloween is over with, but there's always someone who doesn't get the word. Don't worry. You're all right now."

That night Lewis lay wide awake in his bed, listening to his heart beat. His closet door was open, and he could see the clothes hanging in a shadowy row. Were they moving? Was something there, behind them?

Lewis thrashed up into a sitting position and frantically fumbled for the switch on his bedside lamp. He felt all over the lamp before he found it, but finally the light came on. There was nothing there. There were no dark shapes waiting to jump at him. None that he could see, at any rate. It was a long time before he could bring himself to get out of bed and look in the closet. Finally, though, he did. There was nothing behind the clothes. Nothing but plaster and wood and dust and his old shoes. Lewis went back to bed. He thought that maybe he would try to sleep with the light on, tonight.

Lewis tossed and turned. He rolled over to one side and then to the other. It was no good. He wasn't going to sleep. Well, if he wasn't going to sleep, he might as well think. He didn't have to think very hard. Lewis knew very well what was behind all the weird things that had been happening to him lately. The amulet. All his logical explanations had evaporated, and he was left with one thought: the amulet was haunted. It was haunted, and he had better get rid of it. So what if it had helped him beat up on Woody Mingo? So what if it did give him that wonderful pirate-movie feeling? Lewis thought about how he had felt when his hand closed around the amulet and the dark figure leaped at him. He shuddered. He just had to get rid of it.

Lewis raised his hands to his neck. But when they were a few inches away from the chain, they stopped. He grunted and pushed, but he couldn't force them to go any farther. His hands trembled. They shook like the hands of an old man who has the palsy. But they just would not close around the chain so that Lewis could take the amulet off.

Lewis sat up, panting. His pajama top was soaked with sweat. He looked at his hands. Didn't they belong to him any more? Lewis was scared. Thoroughly scared. And he felt helpless. What would he do if he couldn't take it off? He imagined the amulet and chain growing into his body as he got older and older until there was just a looped line and a bump on his skin to show where they were. Lewis's fear was close to panic now. He jumped out of bed and started pacing up and down the room. He would have to calm down before he could decide what to do.

He looked toward the fireplace, and he smiled. Every room in this enormous old mansion had a fireplace in it. Lewis's own personal fireplace was made of black marble, and there was a fire laid in it, though it was not lit. Little dry twigs underneath and bigger sticks above, on the andirons. There was a box of matches on the mantel. Lewis took them and knelt down to light the fire.

In a few minutes, he had a good blaze going. Lewis put up the screen and sat there on the rug, staring at the fire. Should he tell Uncle Jonathan about the amulet? Jonathan was a wizard. He would know what to do. Or Mrs. Zimmermann? She was a witch, and even more powerful than Jonathan. But Lewis was afraid of what they would think when they found out that he had been messing around with magic again. He should have turned Mrs. Zimmermann's book over to her the minute he found it. When she found out what he had done, she would probably be furious. And what would Jonathan do? Would he decide that one year was a long enough time to be Lewis's legal guardian? Would he send him off to live with Uncle Jimmy and Aunt Helen? Aunt Helen had a personality like a leaky inner tube. She sat in an easy chair and whined about her asthma all day. Lewis thought about what life with Aunt Helen would be like. No, he did not want to tell Jonathan and Mrs. Zimmermann about the amulet.

Then who could he tell? Rose Rita. Lewis grinned. Sure. He would call her up in the morning and they could get together to decide what to do. If he couldn't take the amulet off himself, then Rose Rita could do it for him.

The fire crackled cheerfully. Lewis felt better. He also felt very sleepy. After making sure that the fire screen was in place, Lewis stumbled off to the bed and threw himself down. If he had any dreams that night, he didn't remember them.

CHAPTER EIGHT

When he woke up the next morning, Lewis found his room filled with bright winter sunlight. The dark figure that had waited for him under the street lamp seemed like something he had read about or dreamed about. As he dressed, the pirate-movie feeling flowed back into him. He felt like a million dollars. Should he tell Rose Rita, after all? Lewis hesitated. Yes, maybe he ought to, just to get it off his chest. He could call her up before breakfast to catch her before she left the house. But when he got to the phone, Lewis's resolve melted. He stood there with the receiver in his hand while the operator said, "Number please? Number please?" and then he hung up. Oh well. He could talk to her at school.

Lewis saw Rose Rita several times that day at school. But each time, as he was working himself up to say something about the amulet, something tightened up inside him, and he wound up talking about the Notre Dame football team, or the galley they were building, or Miss Haggerty, or anything but the amulet. When he went home from school that day, Lewis still had not managed to tell Rose Rita what he wanted to tell her. But as he walked home in the winter dusk, Lewis saw that the street lights were on. He stopped. Beads of sweat were breaking out on his forehead. The horror of the figure under the lamp swept over him like an icy wave. Lewis pulled himself together. He clenched his teeth and doubled his fists. He was going to have to tell Rose Rita about the amulet, and he was going to tell her tonight.

That evening in the middle of dinner, Lewis laid down his fork, swallowed several times, and said in a dry husky voice, "Uncle Jonathan, can I invite Rose Rita over to stay tonight?"

Jonathan did a double take. "Hmph! Well, Lewis, this is rather short notice, but I'll see what I can do. I'll have to ask her mother's permission first."

After dinner, Jonathan phoned up Mrs. Pottinger, and got her permission for Rose Rita to spend the night over at the Barnavelts' house. Quite by accident, Jonathan discovered that Lewis had not yet asked Rose Rita if she wanted to come over. So he dragged Lewis to the phone and got him to make a formal invitation. Then everything was settled. Lewis and Jonathan went upstairs to one of the many spare bedrooms and made the bed, and laid out the guest towels. Lewis was excited. He was looking forward to a long evening of card games and stories and conversation. Maybe he could even get in a word about his amulet.

When Rose Rita got to Lewis's house, the dining room table was all laid out for poker. There were the blue and gold cards with CAPHARNAUM COUNTY MAGICIANS SOCIETY stamped on them; there were the foreign coins that Jonathan used as poker chips. On a plate with a bright purple border was a big pile of chocolate-chip cookies, and there was a pitcher of milk. Mrs. Zimmermann was there, and she promised not to pull any funny business with the cards. Everything was ready.

They played for a long time. Then, just as Jonathan was about to announce that it was bedtime, Lewis asked if he could have a few words with Rose Rita, alone in the library. As he asked this, Lewis felt that tightness in his chest again. And he felt a sharp pain right where the amulet was.

Jonathan chuckled and knocked his pipe out into the potted plant behind his chair. "Sure," he said. "Sure, go right ahead. State secrets, eh?"

"Yeah, kinda," said Lewis, blushing.

Lewis and Rose Rita went into the library and slid the heavy paneled doors shut. Now Lewis felt like somebody who is trying to breathe under water. But he dragged the words out, one by one.

"Rose Rita?"

"Yeah? What's wrong with you, Lewis? You look all pale."

"Rose Rita, remember when we said the . . . the magic words over the coin?" Lewis stopped and winced. He felt a sharp pain in his chest.

Rose Rita looked puzzled. "Yeah, I remember. What about it?"

Lewis felt as if someone was sticking red-hot needles into his chest. "Well, I . . . I kind of lied about it." Sweat was pouring down his face now, but he felt triumphant, because he was winning over whatever was trying to keep him from telling the truth.

Rose Rita's eyes opened wide. "You lied? You mean the coin was really . . . "

"Yeah." Lewis reached inside his shirt and brought the thing out for her to see. He expected it to be red-hot. But it felt cool to his touch, and it looked just the way it had always looked.

Now that he had gotten out the important part, Lewis found that he could talk more freely. He told Rose Rita about how he had punched Woody without meaning to; he told her about the postcard and the paper on the street, and the figure under the street lamp. Now it was like running downhill. He talked faster and faster until he had nothing more to say.

Rose Rita sat there, nodding and listening, through his

whole speech. When he was through, she said, "Gee, Lewis, don't you think we ought to tell your uncle and Mrs. Zimmermann? They know all about stuff like this."

Lewis looked terrified. "Please don't, Rose Rita! Please, please, don't! My uncle would get mad and bawl me out and . . . and I don't know what he and Mrs. Zimmermann would think! They told me never to mess around with magic again! Please don't say anything to them!"

Rose Rita had not known Lewis long, but she did know that he spent a great deal of time worrying about being bawled out. He worried about it even when he wasn't doing anything bad. And she didn't really know how Jonathan would react. Maybe he *would* lose his temper. So she shrugged and said, "Oh, okay! We won't tell them then. But I think you ought to give the darned thing to me so I can throw it down the sewer for you."

Lewis looked hesitant. He bit his lip. "Could we just maybe . . . kind of put it away for a while? You never know. When I grow up, it might be that I could do something with it."

Rose Rita looked at him over the tops of her glasses. "Like fly to the moon? Come on, Lewis! Stop kidding around. You just want to hang onto it. Give it here." She held out her hand.

Lewis's face suddenly grew hard. He stuffed the coin back in under his shirt. "No."

Rose Rita looked at him for a moment. Then she took off her glasses, folded them up, and put them in the holder in her shirt pocket. She jumped at him, and at the first lunge, got her hands around the chain that the coin was attached to.

Lewis got his hands on the chain too, and he struggled to keep it down around his neck. He fought hard, and Rose Rita was amazed at his strength. She had Indian-wrestled with him once, and she had won easily. But now it was different. They staggered back and forth across the floor of the library. Rose Rita's face got red; so did Lewis's. Neither of them said a word.

Finally Rose Rita gave one sharp yank and tore the chain through Lewis's sore fingers. And at that Lewis gave a wild yell and leaped at her. His hand raked down the side of her face. Blood flowed.

Rose Rita stood in the middle of the room, panting. In one hand she held the chain with the coin on it. With the other she gently touched the wetness on her cheek. Now that the coin was gone, Lewis felt as if he had just been shaken rudely out of a dream. He blinked and stared at Rose Rita and he felt ashamed. Tears came to his eyes.

"Gee, I'm sorry, I didn't mean to. I didn't mean to," was all he could say.

The study doors rolled back, and there was Jonathan. "Good lord, what's going on here? I heard this scream, and I thought someone was being killed!"

Rose Rita hastily stuffed the coin and chain into the pocket of her jeans. "Oh, it wasn't anything, Mr. Barnavelt. Lewis borrowed my Captain Midnight Secret Decoder Ring, and I said that he had kept it long enough, and we had a fight about it."

When she turned to face him, Jonathan saw Rose Rita's bloody cheek. "Wasn't anything? Wasn't anything? Did Lewis do that to you?" Jonathan turned to Lewis, and was on the point of giving him an angry lecture, when Rose Rita interrupted.

"It wasn't what you think, Mr. Barnavelt. I . . . I was scratching my face with the hook end of my glasses. You know, the part that fits down over your ear? Well, it must've gotten sharp somehow because it really gave me a scratch!" Rose Rita was very good at explanations on short notice. Lewis was grateful.

Jonathan looked from Lewis to Rose Rita. There was something fishy about all this, but he couldn't quite tell what. He thought about all the fights he had had with his best friend in grade school, and he smiled. "Oh well. As long as everything's all right."

Late that night, after everyone else was asleep, Rose Rita tiptoed downstairs and opened the front door. She was wearing only her slippers, pajamas, and bathrobe, but she went out anyway, down the shoveled walk and out the front gate. She walked to the corner and stopped by the iron grate of the storm sewer. Water from the melting snow was running down into it with a hollow chuckling sound. Rose Rita took the amulet out of her bathrobe pocket. She dangled it over the grate, swing-

ing it on its chain. All she had to do was let go, and it would be good-bye amulet.

But she didn't let go. A suggestion that seemed to come from outside told her that she shouldn't throw the thing away. Rose Rita stood there a minute, staring at the strange little object that had given Lewis so much trouble. She scooped the coin back into her hand and put it into her bathrobe pocket. As she turned back toward the house, she thought, "Maybe Lewis is right after all. We'll put it away for a while and see what happens. I'll tell him that I've thrown it away, so he won't be pestering me all the time about it. Maybe he can use it when he's older. He might be a great magician or something then. I'll guard it for him." She reached into her pocket to see if the coin was still there. Yes, it was still there. Halfway back to the house she stopped to check again. Then she laughed at herself for being such a fussbudget. She tromped up the creaky steps and went in to bed.

CHAPTER NINE

It was December now, and everyone in New Zebedee was getting ready for Christmas. Big tinsel-covered bells were strung across Main Street in several places, and the fountain at the traffic circle was turned into a Nativity scene. Jonathan lugged the Seagram's and Oxydol boxes down from the attic and began unsnarling the Christmas tree lights. They had been put away in neat little bundles, but they had somehow gotten all knotted up while lying quiet in their boxes. It happened that way every year. Jonathan and Mrs. Zimmermann began their usual argument about which was better, a tall skinny tree or a short squat one. Lewis unpacked the dirty cotton batting and arranged it around the circular mirror that was supposed to be the ice pond. He set up the little cardboard village with the cellophane windows and put the celluloid deer out on the ice. Then, when the tree was all decorated and the lights were turned on, Lewis would sit on the couch and squint. He did this to make the tree lights into stars. Red and blue and green and white and orange stars, each with four long rays. Lewis liked the effect, and he would sit there squinting for long periods of time.

Every night as he undressed for bed, Lewis would look at the green streak on his neck. It had been left there by the tarnished chain that held the magic three-cent piece. The magic amulet that was gone forever. He knew it was gone; Rose Rita had told him so. She had told him that she had dropped it down the sewer, and he had believed her. Now he was trying hard to feel good about not having the amulet. He was trying hard, but it was no use.

Lewis felt the way people feel when they give up something they like. Something that is bad for them, like Mounds bars or eating between meals. He felt a big empty space in his life, a hollow place cut out of his insides. Sometimes he woke up in the middle of the night scrabbling frantically for the amulet. And when he found it wasn't there, he burst into tears. But Lewis went about his everyday life as well as he could. He was distracted from his troubles by the Christmas preparations, and the fun he had playing with Rose Rita. He was happy a good deal of the time, and he might have eventually forgotten all about the amulet if something bad hadn't happened to him.

It was a dark December afternoon. Lewis and the other sixth-grade students were trying very hard to finish their math assignments, so they could be let out early. Miss Haggerty walked up and down the aisles, looking at papers and offering comments. When she was on the other side of the room, Woody Mingo started pinching Lewis.

"Ow!" Lewis hissed. "Cut it out, Woody!"

"Cut out what?"

"You know what I mean. Stop pinchin' me!"

"I ain't pinchin' you. It must be a sweat bee. Take a bath, and they won't sting you. Sweat Bee Barney-smell, Sweat Bee Barney-smell." Pinch, pinch.

Lewis felt deep despair. It was as if Woody had begun to realize that the amulet was gone. For a long time after their big fight, Woody had let Lewis alone. But in the last few days he had started in again. It was worse than before.

Lewis wanted to slug Woody, but he knew he'd get caught if he tried anything. Besides, he wasn't sure he could hurt Woody at all without his amulet. *Why did he ever agree to give it away?* It was one of the dumbest things he had ever done in his life.

Miss Haggerty walked to the front of the room and picked up her watch.

"Class," she said.

Everyone stopped working and looked up.

"Since you all seem to be doing quite well, I will keep my promise and let you out early. Some of you are not quite finished, but you may complete your work at home. Now, as soon as you have your desks all cleared off, and the room is quiet, you may go."

Desk tops slammed all over the room as the students began stuffing their pencils, paper, and books into their desks. Lewis put all his books away, and then he started stuffing his pens and pencils down the hole that the ink bottle sat in.

The students in Lewis's school didn't get to use ballpoint pens. Not in school, at any rate. Ballpoint pens were supposed to be bad for your handwriting. So everybody had to write either with fountain pens, or with wooden pens, the kind that have metal points on the end. The ink the students used was kept in glass bottles which sat in round holes that had been cut in the upper-right-hand corner of each desk top. The holes went right through to the inside of the desk, so if you took the bottle out, you could put things into your desk through the hole. Of course, it would really have been easier just to lift the hinged wooden lid of the desk, but you couldn't have told Lewis that.

Lewis had about four pencils and a pen crammed into the hole. They were stuck against some books that were inside his desk, and they wouldn't go in. With his left hand he jiggled them around, trying to force them in. In his right hand he held the ink bottle. It dangled out over the aisle. Suddenly something hit Lewis's arm. Right on the funny bone. His arm went numb, his hand went limp, and the ink bottle shattered on the floor. Black ink spattered everywhere.

Lewis turned angrily in his seat. Woody was just pulling himself hastily back behind his raised desk top. And now Miss Haggerty was standing next to Lewis's desk.

"What seems to be the matter here?"

"Woody knocked the ink out of my hand," said Lewis, pointing.

Miss Haggerty did not seem to be interested in Woody. She kept on staring at Lewis. "And what, may I ask, was the ink bottle doing in your hand, Mr. Barnavelt?"

Lewis blushed. "I was just puttin' my pencils down into the hole," he mumbled.

The room was quiet. Dead quiet. Everyone, including Rose Rita, was looking at Lewis.

Miss Haggerty turned to the class and said, in a loud clear voice, "Class, do we *ever* take our ink bottles out of our desks?"

The class answered in long drawn-out unison. "NO-O, MISS HAG-GER-TY!"

Lewis's face burned. He felt angry and helpless. Now he heard Miss Haggerty telling him that he would have to stay after school and sand some of the ink off the floor. She didn't say how long it would take.

An hour after everyone else had gone, Miss Haggerty let Lewis go. His fingertips were sore from sandpapering, and he was so mad he could hardly see straight. As he stomped along the sidewalk toward home, he felt mad at everybody and everything, but especially at Rose Rita. It didn't matter that she had come over to his desk when the class was let out, just to say that she was sorry he had to stay after and to tell him that she hadn't chanted "No, Miss Haggerty" along with the rest of the class. That didn't matter. He was mad at her, and he felt that he had a very good reason.

If he had had the amulet with him in school that day, Lewis figured, it would have protected him. Woody would have been afraid to pick on him. The ink bottle would never have gotten broken, and he would never have been forced to stay after school. And who had told him to get rid of the amulet? Rose Rita. As Lewis saw it, everything that had happened to him that day was Rose Rita's fault.

The more Lewis walked, the madder he got. Why did Rose Rita have to butt in on everything, anyway? If only he could get the amulet back! But how could he? It was gone forever, down the storm sewer. By now it had been washed out into Wilder Creek and maybe even into Lake Michigan. It was no use . . .

Lewis stopped dead in the middle of the street. He happened to be crossing a busy intersection at the time, so cars honked at him and drivers put on their brakes in a hurry to avoid hitting him. Lewis heard the brakes screeching and the horns honking, and he broke out of his trance long enough to get safely across the street. But when he was on the other side, he went right on thinking the thought that had made him stop.

What if Rose Rita still had the amulet? What if she had been lying when she said she dropped it down the sewer?

The longer Lewis thought about it, the more certain he was that his wild guess was right. After all, he hadn't actually *seen* her drop the amulet down the drain. Maybe he had better try to get some information out of her.

On Friday of that week, a boiler burst in the basement of Lewis's school. Everybody got out early. Lewis and Rose Rita decided that they would spend the afternoon working on the Roman galley. It was nearly finished, but it needed a few final touches.

The galley stood in the middle of Rose Rita's desk up in her room. Around it were balsa wood shavings, bits of cardboard, and globs of dried model airplane glue. Lewis sat at Rose Rita's desk, hacking at a strip of balsa wood with his Boy Scout knife. He was trying to make a fancy battering ram to go on the prow of the ship.

"Gosh darn!" Lewis threw the jacknife down and glared at it.

Rose Rita looked up from the book she was leafing through. "What's wrong?"

"Oh, it's just this darned old knife. It wouldn't cut butter."

Rose Rita thought a minute. "Hey!" she said, "why don't we get out my Exacto knives? I forgot all about them. They're in my bureau drawer."

"Great! Which drawer are they in? I'll get them out." Lewis pushed his chair back and got up. He went to the dresser and started opening drawers and looking into them.

Rose Rita jumped up and ran to stop him. "Come on, Lewis! Hands off! That's my bureau, and my own private stuff is in there! And besides," she added, grinning, "you couldn't get into the right drawer anyway. It's locked, and I've got the only key to it, and I'm *not* going to tell you where it is. Now, go out and stand in the hall and close the door behind you. It'll only take a minute."

"Oh, okay!" Lewis grumbled. He stomped out into the hall and slammed the door behind him. As he stood there staring at the wallpaper, he thought, "Own private stuff, huh? I'll bet that's where you've got my amulet, right in there with your own private stuff. But don't worry, I'll get it back!"

A few minutes later, Rose Rita let Lewis come back into the room. The bureau drawers were all closed as before, but the Exacto knives were laid out on the desk. Lewis looked the tall black bureau up and down. Which drawer was it? It had to be one of the two up at the top,

because they were the only ones that had locks. But how was he going to get in without a key?

Rose Rita saw how Lewis was eyeing the bureau, and she began to get worried. "Come on, Lewis," she said, taking him by the arm. "There's nothing in there but my own stuff. Some of it I won't even let my mom look at, so don't feel too left out. Hey, let's get to work on the galley. Here, this is how the blades fit on the holders. . . ."

Late that night, Lewis lay awake, tossing and turning. He heard the grandfather clock in the study downstairs thud one o'clock, and then two, and then three. Lewis was trying to put together a plan for getting a look in the locked drawers of Rose Rita's bureau. But it was no use. Everything depended on his having the key, and he didn't have the faintest idea of where to look for it. He thought of ransacking her room some time when she was out, but he didn't see how he could do that without attracting her mother's attention. And he didn't want to make a mess. Everything would have to be done carefully and secretly, so Rose Rita would not realize what was going on. Lewis was hoping that the amulet would be tucked away in some dark corner of one of those two drawers, some place that Rose Rita didn't look at very often. Lewis grimaced. Maybe Rose Rita checked the bureau every day, just to see if the amulet was there. Maybe he could have a fake one made . . . no, that sounded impossible. If he got the amulet away from her, and she found out about it, it would just be too darned bad.

But how was he going to get it? Lewis thought about skeleton keys and midnight break-ins with rope ladders and black masks and tool bags and the works. Then he thought, "Gee, what if it's not in her bureau at all? What if she really did throw it away?" In any case, he wasn't going to find out anything without the key to the drawer. And he didn't even know where to look for it.

Lewis got that hopeless feeling. As the clock struck four, he drifted off to sleep. That night, Lewis dreamed about keys. He was wandering through the many rooms of an old junk shop, and every room was full to the ceiling with keys. Keys of all sizes and shapes. Some of them were hooked together on rings, but most were just piled loose on the floor. He searched and searched, but he couldn't find the one he wanted.

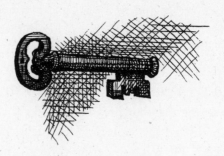

CHAPTER TEN

When Lewis woke up the next morning, he was still thinking about keys. But he wasn't any closer to finding the key to Rose Rita's bureau drawer. It was Saturday, and Rose Rita had an appointment to see her eye doctor. She was nearsighted, and her eyes were changing fast, so she had to get her glasses changed often. Lewis was going along with her today, to have his eyes examined. He didn't wear glasses, but Jonathan had noticed that Lewis was falling asleep over books a good deal, and he wondered if Lewis didn't need reading glasses. Lewis had protested, but finally he had agreed to go.

That afternoon Lewis and Rose Rita were sitting in Dr. Wessel's office, reading comic books. Lewis had just finished having his eyes examined. It was Rose Rita's turn now.

Dr. Wessel opened his office door and peered out into the waiting room. "Okay. Who's next?"

Rose Rita threw her comic book down and got up. "I guess I am," she said wearily. "See you later, Lewis."

As she got up to go in, Lewis noticed that she was still wearing her beanie. That darned beanie! She wore it everywhere. To church, in school, at dinner, and she probably even wore it in bed at night. It was weird.

Lewis went back to his comic book, but he was startled a few seconds later when he heard loud voices. Rose Rita and Dr. Wessel were having an argument behind the closed door. Suddenly Dr. Wessel jerked the door open and pointed at the hat rack by the mirror.

"There!" he said, firmly. "Put it there!"

"I don't want to! Who do you think you are? God?"

Dr. Wessel glowered at Rose Rita. "No, I'm not God. I'm just a crabby eye doctor, and I don't want you wearing that beanie while I'm testing your eyes. It bumps into my equipment, and it distracts me, and . . . well, I don't like it. Now hang it up out there, or go on home."

"Oh, all right!" Rose Rita stormed out into the waiting room and jammed her beanie onto one of the pegs of the hat rack. Then she marched back into Dr. Wessel's office. He closed the door quietly behind her.

Lewis glanced up at the beanie and grinned. Rose Rita sure was funny about it. He picked up his comic book and then, quite suddenly, he laid it down again.

What if the key was in the beanie?

Lewis got up and walked softly over to the hat rack. Carefully, he lifted the beanie down. He looked inside, and there, held to the cloth by a safety pin, was a small black key.

Lewis felt like cheering. It had to be the right key, it just had to be. He glanced nervously at the closed door of Dr. Wessel's office. How much time did he have? He had heard Rose Rita say that her sessions with Dr. Wessel took quite a while, because there were lots of things wrong with her eyes. Would she be in there for a whole hour? Lewis looked at the clock. He'd just have to chance it. He undid the safety pin, put the key in his pocket, put the pin back in the hat again, snapped it shut, and carefully put the beanie back. He hoped Rose Rita wouldn't hear the buttons on the beanie rattling. When he had done all this, Lewis stepped over to the office door and rapped on it.

"Rose Rita?"

"Yeah?"

"I . . . I just remembered that I have to go downtown and buy some tobacco for Uncle Jonathan. It'll only take a couple of minutes."

"Oh, take all the time you want! I'm likely to be in here for days."

"Uh . . . okay. I'll be right back."

Lewis struggled into his coat and hat and galoshes, and stumbled down the front steps of Dr. Wessel's office. Soon he was walking as fast as he could toward Rose Rita's house. His hand was closed around the cold key in his pocket, and as he walked, he planned. He had to think up something to say to Mrs. Pottinger.

When Lewis got to the front steps of the Pottinger house, he took a deep breath. Then he went up and rang the bell. After what seemed like a very long time, Mrs. Pottinger came to the door. She was surprised to see him.

"Why, Lewis! What are you doing here? I thought you were at Dr. Wessel's office with Rose Rita."

Lewis dug his hands into his pockets and stared at the doormat. "Well, yeah, I kinda was, but it's like this: Rose Rita and I were gonna go to Heemsoth's for a Coke afterwards, and I don't have enough money, and she said she left her wallet up on top of her dresser. Can I go get it?"

It seemed to Lewis as if thousands of years were passing between the time he finished this speech and the time Mrs. Pottinger gave her answer. He began to wonder if kids who were caught burgling other kids' bureaus got sent to the Detention Home.

Mrs. Pottinger did take a little while to answer him, because she was an absent-minded person. "Why, yes, I suppose it's all right," she said, at last. "If you had said it was *in* the bureau, I'd have said you were out of luck, because Rose Rita won't even let me poke around in there. Go ahead. If you can't find the wallet, I think I have some money."

"Gee, thanks a lot, Mrs. Pottinger. I'll just be a minute."

"Take your time." Mrs. Pottinger turned and walked back toward the kitchen. Lewis watched her go. She trusted him. And why shouldn't she? He was Rose Rita's best friend. He felt awful. He wanted to go hide in a cellar somewhere. But instead, he started up the stairs.

Lewis stood before the bureau with the key in his hand. He listened, expecting at any minute to hear Mrs. Pottinger's footstep on the stairs. But instead he heard the clatter and clink of the dishes she was washing. He turned and saw that he had left the bedroom door open. Quickly he walked over and closed it. Then he went back to the bureau. The two drawers at the top had locks. It had to be one of them. Probably the same key fitted both locks. At least, he hoped it did. Lewis decided to try the right-hand drawer first. He stuck the key in and turned it. But when he pulled, he found that the drawer wouldn't budge. Which meant that the drawer hadn't been locked in the first place. Lewis turned the key back the other way and slid the drawer out. It was stuffed full of Rose Rita's underwear. Lewis felt his face getting red. He slid the drawer back. The amulet might be in there, but he would check the other drawer first.

Lewis unlocked the left-hand drawer and slid it out. It was full of little boxes and junk. This had to be the right one. He took the drawer all the way out, set it on Rose Rita's desk, and started going through it. But just as he was opening the first box, Lewis heard a knock on the door.

"Everything all right in there?"

Lewis froze. Mr. Pottinger! He had forgotten all about him! Usually, Mr. Pottinger wasn't home during the day. But this was Saturday. He was out there in the hall, on the other side of the door, waiting for an answer. Lewis's mind was racing. What should he do? Answer? Or try to climb out the window?

Another knock. Sharper and more insistent than before. And then Lewis heard Mr. Pottinger's loud, resonant voice again. "I *said*, is everything all *right* in there?"

Lewis glanced wildy around. His glance fell on the doorknob. He was fascinated by it. It would start to turn at any minute, and then . . .

Lewis heard Mrs. Pottinger calling from the foot of the stairs. "For heaven's sake, calm down, George! It's just Lewis Barnavelt looking for Rose Rita's wallet."

"Well then why doesn't he answer me? I heard this noise in her room, and I knew she was out, so I wondered . . ."

"Well, stop wondering, and leave the poor boy alone. He didn't answer you because he's shy, and you scared him to death with all that bellowing. You were shy too once. I should think you'd remember that!"

Mr. Pottinger chuckled. "Yeah, I guess I was." He gave a light playful tap on the door and said, "Good hunting, Lewis!" Then he walked on down the hall, humming to himself. A door closed, and Lewis heard Mr. Pottinger running water in the bathroom.

Lewis was standing there by the desk with the lid of the Exacto blade box in his hands. He was shaking all over. When he finally got himself pulled back together, he went back to examining the contents of the drawer. A box of Exacto blades. A chestnut carved to look like a jack-o-lantern. A deck of miniature playing cards in a cardboard case. The case said "Little Duke Toy Cards." One by one Lewis took the things out and laid them on the green blotter. No amulet yet.

A box of little plastic chessmen with the label "Drueke" on the top. A pair of magnetic toys shaped like the Republican elephant and the Democratic donkey. And then a worn little blue case with "Marshall Field's, Chicago" stamped on it. A white address label had been pasted on under the Marshall Field's label. It said: "Miss Rose Rita Pottinger, 39 Mansion Street, New Zebedee, Michigan." Lewis opened the box and saw his amulet.

Lewis could hardly believe it. Tears came to his eyes. It was really there! With trembling fingers he picked up the chain and slipped it over his head. Then he buttoned the top button of his shirt. Lewis hated tight collars, and this button, which he had never done up before in his life, felt like it was choking him. But it didn't matter. He had to go back and face Rose Rita, and he didn't want her to see the chain around his neck.

Lewis stopped and listened. He couldn't tell very well with the door shut, but it sounded like Mrs. Pottinger was singing downstairs. She often sang while she did the dishes or the dusting. And the sound of running water continued. Mr. Pottinger was probably taking a bath. Good. Now he would have to get out as fast as he could.

Working quickly, Lewis began putting the various items back in Rose Rita's drawer. He hoped that she hadn't put them in some particular order, so that she could find out if somebody had been fooling around with her stuff. Well, if she had, it was just too bad. Some day she would look and find that the amulet was gone, but by then she would understand why he had had to take it. He would protect her with his strength and bravery. Lewis hoped that this was the way it would all turn out.

Lewis put the drawer back in place and turned the key in the lock. There! Now he could leave. He would just go back to Dr. Wessel's office and put the key back in the beanie and sit down to wait for Rose Rita as if nothing had happened.

Humming quietly to himself, Lewis walked down the hall and trotted down the stairs. He had just laid his hand on the knob of the front door when Mrs. Pottinger called from the kitchen. "Did you get what you wanted, Lewis?"

"Uh . . . yeah. Gee, thanks a lot. Bye." Lewis's voice was so high that it was practically a squeak. He was very nervous. Now the door had closed behind him. He was outside. He had gotten away with it. He could be strong now, without the aid of Charles Atlas or punching bags or anything.

But on the steps of the Pottingers' house, Lewis paused. He was thinking of the black figure. Would it come back, now that he had the amulet? This fear had been in the back of Lewis's mind ever since he began plotting to get the magic coin back. Lewis had kept the fear down with his usual "logical explanations." But it was still there.

"Oh heck," he said, out loud. "I'm just being a scaredy-cat. Nobody can hurt me now." For the fifteenth time, Lewis persuaded himself that the figure that had jumped at him outside the library was just some crazy guy. Every now and then they got loose from the Kalamazoo Mental Hospital, and they would do things like jump out naked from behind trees and scare people at night until the police caught them and put them back in the crazy house. That was who it had been under the street lamp. Some nut.

Lewis glanced up at the sky. It was getting dark. He decided that he'd better be getting back before Rose

Rita suspected that something was up. He buttoned his coat and started out.

As Lewis walked back along Mansion Street, it started to snow. Little white flakes whirled around him and stung his face. He felt funny, as if he didn't know where he was going. The familiar shapes of cars rolled by in the early winter dusk, but they seemed to Lewis like bug-eyed prehistoric monsters. Maybe there was a blizzard coming. Well, that was okay with Lewis. He would enjoy sitting by the fire in Jonathan's library, with a steaming cup of cocoa in his hand. He would watch the snow falling outside the window. It would be very cozy.

Lewis kicked his way through the snow that was piling up on the sidewalk. Little glittering spurts rose before him. Now he was passing the Masonic Temple, a tall four-story brick building. It rose over him like a black cliff. There was a dark archway in the front of the building. For some reason, Lewis stopped in front of it. He didn't know why. He just stopped and waited.

Now Lewis heard something. A rustling sound. An old newspaper blew out of the archway. It slithered toward him like a living thing. Lewis was frightened, but then he tried to laugh it away. What was there to be scared of in an old newspaper? It lay at his feet now. He bent over and picked it up. By the light of the lamp that was swinging in the wind at the corner, Lewis could

just barely read the masthead. It was the New Zebedee *Chronicle*, and the date was April 30, 1859. The date on the three-cent piece was 1859.

With a little cry of terror, Lewis let go of the paper. It refused to go, however. Like a friendly cat, the paper wrapped itself around his feet. Frantically, Lewis kicked at the thing. He wanted it to go away. But then he stopped kicking. He turned and looked toward the dark archway. A figure stepped forward from it.

Lewis opened and closed his mouth, but nothing came out. He wanted to say, "Oh, hi there, Joe!" to reassure himself, but he couldn't. Rooted to the spot, Lewis watched the figure come. A breath of cold ashes swept toward him.

Now the figure was standing before Lewis on the snowy walk. It raised a shadowy hand and motioned for him to come. And Lewis felt himself suddenly jolted forward. It was as if there was a dog collar around his neck and the figure was tugging at the leash. He couldn't resist. He had to go. Lewis stumbled forward, following the beckoning shape. The snow closed in and hid them both from sight.

CHAPTER ELEVEN

Rose Rita glanced up at the clock in the waiting room of Dr. Wessel's office. It was the third time she had looked at it in the last five minutes.

The clock said five-fifteen. Lewis had left the office at three-thirty or thereabouts. It was hard to believe that it had taken him nearly two hours to buy a can of tobacco, go home, and then come back. Except, of course, that he hadn't come back. No phone calls, no nothing. Rose Rita's session with Dr. Wessel hadn't taken too long. She had been sitting out in the waiting room stewing for more than an hour now, and she was just about fed up.

Rose Rita stormed out into the front hall and started

throwing on her outdoor clothes. Coat, scarf, boots, gloves. Boy, was she mad! She kept running through in her mind all the things she was going to say to Lewis when she saw him again. She reached up and snatched down her beanie. As she always did, she stuck her hand inside to see if the key was there. It was gone.

Rose Rita stood there staring at the safety pin that had held the little key. So *that* was what he was up to! Why, the dirty, sneaky, crooked, no-good . . . She felt more anger welling up inside her, making her even crabbier than she had been before. But then she stopped. Lewis had told her all about the amulet, about the figure waiting for him under the lamp and the ghostly messages that had come floating in out of nowhere. He had gone to get the amulet, and he had not come back.

Rose Rita opened the front door of Dr. Wessel's office and looked out. It was dark and it was snowing. She fought down her rising panic and said to herself, through clenched teeth, "I've got to get help. I've got to get help." Still saying this over and over, she hurried down the steps and started kicking her way through the snow.

Lewis's Uncle Jonathan was winding the mantel clock in the dining room when he heard a terrific hammering on the front door. When he got there, he found Rose Rita, red-faced, panting, and covered with snow.

"Mr. Barnavelt . . . Mr. Barnavelt . . . it's . . . we've got to . . . too late . . . took him . . . go find him . . ." Cold wet

bubbles were rising from Rose Rita's throat and bursting in her mouth. She couldn't talk any more.

Jonathan put his arm around her and tried to make her calm down. He told her that she'd better get out of that heavy wet coat. But when he tried to help her unbutton her parka, she shoved him away angrily. Rose Rita stood there trying to catch her breath. It took her some time. When she finally got her voice back, she stared straight at Jonathan and spoke as calmly as she could.

"Mr. Barnavelt . . . there's . . . there's something awful's happened to Lewis. You know that old coin you gave him . . . out of your grampa's trunk?"

Jonathan gave Rose Rita a strange look. "Yes, I remember. What about it?"

"Well, it's magic, and he took it away from me and now it's got him and we've got to . . ." Rose Rita broke down. She put her hands to her face and cried. Her whole body shook.

Several minutes later, Rose Rita and Jonathan and Mrs. Zimmermann were sitting around the kitchen table in Mrs. Zimmermann's house. Mrs. Zimmermann was holding Rose Rita's hand and comforting her. Rose Rita had just finished telling them both the whole story, as far as she knew it.

"Don't worry, Rose Rita," Mrs. Zimmermann said softly. "Everything'll be all right. We'll find him."

Rose Rita stopped crying and looked her straight in the eye. "Oh yeah? Well, how're we gonna do it?"

Mrs. Zimmermann stared at the table. "I don't know yet," she said in a low voice.

It was hard for Rose Rita to fight down despair. She wanted them all to jump into the car right away and zoom off in search of Lewis. But they didn't even know which way they ought to go. The kitchen clock fizzed, and Mrs. Zimmermann rapped the large purple stone of her ring on the white enamel of the tabletop. She was trying to think.

Suddenly Mrs. Zimmermann shoved her chair back and jumped up. "Of course! Come on, everybody. Get your things on. I know where we're going now."

Rose Rita and Jonathan were utterly mystified, but they followed Mrs. Zimmermann out to the front hall and started getting dressed. Jonathan put on his big fur coat and the hat that looked like a small black haystack. Mrs. Zimmermann put on her heavy purple cape and rooted in the hall closet until she found her umbrella. It was a small black umbrella with rust streaks running down it and a crystal knob for a handle. Rose Rita wondered why she wanted it.

As soon as everyone was ready, they went next door, and Jonathan got his car out of the garage. Now Rose Rita was squeezed into the front seat between Jonathan and Mrs. Zimmermann. As the car reached the corner of Mansion and High, Jonathan put on the brakes and turned to Rose Rita.

"Okay, Rosie," he said, "I think I'd better take you home now. It's getting late and your folks'll be wondering where you are. And I wouldn't think of taking you along on a dangerous journey like this one."

Rose Rita set her jaw and stared back at Jonathan defiantly. "Mr. Barnavelt, if you want to get rid of me you'll have to tie me up and dump me on my front porch."

Jonathan looked at Rose Rita for a second. Then he shrugged and drove on.

The big black car crawled down Main Street and rounded the traffic circle. The snow was coming down hard. It piled up on the figures of Mary and Joseph inside the columns of the fountain. Rose Rita saw that they were headed out of town now. The CITY LIMITS sign passed. So did the Athletic Field and the Bowl-Mor Bowling Alley. Jonathan had had a hurried consultation with Mrs. Zimmermann just before they left the house, and he seemed to know where they were going. Normally, Rose Rita would have been irritated about not being let in on their little secret. But she was so worried about Lewis that she didn't care where they went, as long as they were going somewhere to save him.

Now they were out in the country. The tire chains chinked steadily, and white dots came rushing out of the blackness. Rose Rita stared at them, hypnotized. She imagined that she was in a space ship plowing through the Asteroid Belt. The dots were meteorites. *Chink-chink* went the chains. *Swish-swish* went the windshield wipers as they slowly cleared the snow away. The white dots kept flying at the car. Rose Rita felt the warm breath of the heater on her legs. Although it was still early in the evening, she felt exhausted. Running through the snow from the doctor's office to Lewis's house had really tired her out. Her head began to fall forward . . .

"It's no use. We can't go any farther."

Rose Rita shook her head and wiped her eyes. "Huh?"

It was Jonathan who had spoken. He put the car into reverse and backed up a bit. Then he put it in first and pressed steadily down on the accelerator. The car rolled forward a little way, but then it stopped. The tires squealed and whined. Jonathan backed up and tried again. And again. And again. Finally, he turned the ignition off. He heaved a deep sigh, ground his teeth, and banged with his fists on the useless steering wheel. Before them on the road stretched a rippled desert of snow. It was too deep for them to drive through.

The car dripped and ticked into silence. White flakes began piling up on the windshield wipers. The three of them sat watching for what seemed like a long time, though it was really less than a minute. Then Mrs. Zimmermann cleared her throat. The sudden sound made

Jonathan and Rose Rita jump. They turned toward her, wondering what she was going to say. Now she thrust her arms through the armholes in her cape and picked her umbrella up off the floor of the car. "All right, everybody out. Buckle up your galoshes and button up your coats. We'll have to walk."

Jonathan stared at her. "*Walk?* Florence, are you crazy? It's still . . . well, how many miles would you say it was?"

"Not as many as you would claim, Weird Beard," said Mrs. Zimmermann, smiling grimly. "But in any case we're wasting time. We've *got* to walk. That's all there is to it." She opened the car door and slid out. Rose Rita followed her. Jonathan shut off the headlights and took the flashlight out of the glove compartment. Soon he was charging off after the other two.

Walking through deep snow is hard work. You have to keep lifting your feet up and down, up and down, out of one hole and into another, until your legs feel like they're going to fall off. It didn't take long for Jonathan, Mrs. Zimmermann, and Rose Rita to get tired out.

"Oh, this is useless!" Jonathan gasped. He tore off his hat and threw it down into the snow. "We'll never get there at this rate!"

"We have to," panted Mrs. Zimmermann. "Rest a minute and we'll go on. At least it's stopped snowing."

It was true. Rose Rita looked up, and she could see

stars. The moon was out too, a big full moon. By its light they could see their car in the distance, just around a bend of the road. They had not yet gotten out of sight of it.

"I have never seen such lazy people as the people in the Capharnaum County Highway Department," Jonathan grumbled. "They should be out here right now with their trucks!"

"Save your breath for walking," said Mrs. Zimmermann.

They started out again. Up and down, up and down, through the glimmering white stuff. Rose Rita began to cry. Her tears felt cold on her cheeks. "We'll never see Lewis again, will we? Will we?" she sobbed. "Not ever again!"

Mrs. Zimmermann didn't answer. Neither did Jonathan. They just kept slogging.

They had walked for what seemed like hours when Jonathan stopped and put his hand to his left side. "Can't ... go ... farther ... hurts ..." he gasped. "Shouldn't ... eat ... so much ..."

Rose Rita looked at Mrs. Zimmermann. She seemed ready to collapse. Now Mrs. Zimmermann turned away and put her hands over her face. Rose Rita knew she must be crying.

"This is the end," Rose Rita thought. "This is the end of everything." But just then she heard a noise in the distance. A growling, scraping, grinding noise. She turned and looked back down the road. Yellow lights were flashing in the distance. A snow plow was coming.

Rose Rita could hardly believe her eyes. Tired as she was, she started jumping up and down and cheering. Mrs. Zimmermann took her hands away from her face and just stood watching. Jonathan picked up his hat, dusted it off, and jammed it back on his head. He blew his nose and wiped his eyes several times. "Well, it's about time!" he said in a hoarse voice.

Now the plow was getting closer. Rose Rita thought she had never seen anything so beautiful in her life. It was a festival of flashing lights and wonderful noises. Sparks flew from the big curved blade. The motor whined and rumbled. They could read the words on the door of the big yellow truck: CAPHARNAUM COUNTY PUBLIC WORKS DEPARTMENT.

Jonathan turned on the flashlight and yelled and waved. With a long grating roar the truck pulled to a stop next to the three travelers. Snow from the plow blade spattered them, but they didn't mind.

A window in the cab was rolled down. "Hey, are you the people that left your car in the middle of the road?"

"Yes we are, and what's it to you, Jute Feasel?" Jonathan roared. "I never was so glad to see anyone in my life! Can you give us a ride?"

"Where to?"

"Halfway up the Homer Road to the old Moss Farm."

"What the hell you want to go out there for?"

"Watch your language, Jute," Mrs. Zimmermann called. "We've got a young lady with us." Rose Rita giggled. It was well known in New Zebedee that Jute Feasel had the foulest mouth in town.

Jute agreed to drive the three of them where they wanted to go. He said he didn't understand it, and Jonathan said he didn't have to, and they left it at that. The cab of the truck was a bit crowded with four people in it, but somehow they all managed to squeeze in. Mrs. Zimmermann sat in the middle, and Rose Rita sat on Jonathan's lap. It was too hot in the cab, and the air was thick with the smell of the King Edward cigars that Jute always smoked. But they were on their way again.

The truck ground up and down hills and around curves, shooting snow in either direction. Jonathan sang "Drill Ye Tarriers" to keep everyone's spirits up. Jute sang the song about the three little fishies in the itty-bitty pool, which was the only song he knew that was fit for children to listen to. Snow-covered trees stared at them from the darkness on both sides of the road.

Finally, in the middle of nowhere, the truck stopped. There was a wire fence, and some trees, and the snow and the moonlight. And that was all.

"Well, here we are!" said Jute. "I don't know what the he . . . er, heck you want out here, but you're old friends, and I'm glad to oblige. You want me to send somebody out to get you?"

"Yes," said Jonathan. "Does that thing work?" He

pointed to a radio on the dashboard. There was a micro-phone attached to it.

"Sure it does."

"Well, then, I want you to phone up Oaklawn Hospital and tell them to send an ambulance out here as fast as they can. No, I'm not going to explain. Thanks, Jute, and we'll see you soon." He opened the door and jumped out of the truck. Mrs. Zimmermann and Rose Rita followed him. As they walked around the front of the truck, Rose Rita looked up and saw Jute's face. It looked green in the light from the dashboard, and it also looked puzzled. Jute was talking into the microphone, giving directions.

"Hey!" shouted Jonathan. "Look at this!" He waved his flashlight excitedly.

Mrs. Zimmermann and Rose Rita followed Jonathan over to the edge of the road. There were holes in the snow. Footprints.

"Wow!" said Rose Rita. "Do you think it's Lewis?" For the first time in hours, she was feeling hopeful.

"Can't tell," said Jonathan, shining the flashlight into the dark holes. "They're half full of snow, but they're about his size. Come on. Let's see where they go."

With Jonathan in the lead, the three of them walked along by the side of the road until they came to a place where the footprints turned toward the fence. It was a barbed-wire fence, about chest-high to a man. A yellow tin sign advertising DeKalb Corn hung from the top strand. It rattled in the freezing wind. Suddenly Jonathan gave a cry and stumbled forward. He flashed the light at the sign. "Look!"

Something was caught on the corner of the sign. Something that fluttered in the wind. A piece of brown corduroy. There was dried blood on it, and there were little dabs of blood on the sign.

"It's Lewis, all right!" said Mrs. Zimmermann. "I don't think he's worn anything but corduroy pants since I've known him. But the blood! He must have cut himself going over the fence."

"Come on," said Jonathan.

Over the fence they went, one at a time. Mrs. Zimmermann was the last one over, and she caught her cape on a barb, but she ripped it loose and hurried on. The footprints went off across a snowy field.

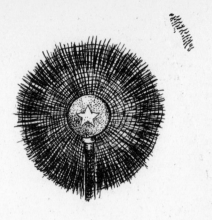

CHAPTER TWELVE

Jonathan, Rose Rita, and Mrs. Zimmermann stumbled across the snow-covered field. They were headed toward a little grove of pine trees. Jonathan was in the lead, and he played the flashlight beam over the footprints they were following, though they could be seen quite clearly by the light of the moon. The ground was uneven under the smooth layer of snow, and every now and then one of the three would stumble and fall. But in spite of this, they pressed on.

As they got closer to the dark grove of trees, each of them had the same feeling about it, though nobody spoke. They all felt that the trees were like a curtain hiding some scene from their eyes. They pushed on into the mass of fragrant boughs and shoved them aside. And there on the other side of the grove, they stopped.

Jonathan, Rose Rita, and Mrs. Zimmermann found that they were standing at the top of a low hill. At the bottom of the hill a wide space had been cleared in the snow. In the center of the patch of bare ground was a large well. Its top lay even with the ground, and nearby lay a heavy stone cover. Lewis stood a few feet away from the lip of the well. And a dark shape stood by the well, beckoning for Lewis to come.

Jonathan, Rose Rita, and Mrs. Zimmermann watched in horror. They could do nothing. Again the figure beckoned. Lewis stiffened. He did not move. Then the figure raised its hand and made a strange sign in the air. Lewis shuffled a few feet closer. Now he was almost at the edge of the well.

"Stop!" cried Mrs. Zimmermann. Her voice was loud and resonant, as if she were speaking under a dome.

Rose Rita turned and looked at her. Mrs. Zimmermann had changed. The folds of her ratty old purple cape were filled with orange light. A pale flickering light played over her homely wrinkled face. And in her hand, instead of an umbrella, she held a tall rod topped by a crystal sphere. Within the sphere a purple star burned. It threw a long violet slash, like a glowing sword, across the snow.

"I command you to stop!" Mrs. Zimmermann shouted again.

The dark shape hesitated. Lewis stood motionless, a few feet from the pit. Then a battle began.

It was like giant flashbulbs going off all over, all at once. It was like thunder, not only overhead but in the air all around and under the earth. Rose Rita fell to her knees in the snow and hid her face. When she raised her eyes again, the world lay in gray moonlight. Lewis had rushed back to the outer edge of the wide circle of snow. But the dark figure was still there by the well. And Mrs. Zimmermann lay crumpled in the snow. Near her lay the twisted wreckage of an old umbrella. The crystal knob had been shattered, as if by the blow of a hammer. Mrs. Zimmermann had lost.

Rose Rita sprang to her feet. She wanted to help Mrs. Zimmermann and help Lewis, to do everything all at once and save everybody. But she couldn't do anything. Jonathan was bending over Mrs. Zimmermann. It looked like he was trying to help her up. Rose Rita whirled frantically and looked down the hill. Lewis was shuffling toward the well once again. The dark figure kept motioning him forward, waving its arms in strange rhythmical gestures. Then Rose Rita heard Mrs. Zimmermann's voice. It was weak and raspy, like the voice of someone who has been sick for a long time.

"Rose Rita! Come over here! Come over here quick!"

Rose Rita thrashed through the snow till she was at Mrs. Zimmermann's side.

"Hold out your hand!" Mrs. Zimmermann barked.

Rose Rita held out her hand. Mrs. Zimmermann reached into her pocket and pulled out what looked like a piece of phosphorescent chalk. When she put it in Rose Rita's hand, it burned like an icicle.

"Take this and go to him! It's our only chance. Go on, run, before it's too late!"

Rose Rita took the thing in her fist and started down the hill. She expected it to be hard going, but it was strange. It seemed as if the snow was giving way in front of her. Before she knew it she was standing in the strange circular clearing. The shadow was still beckoning to Lewis. It took no notice of her.

And now Rose Rita was filled with anger at this horrible creature that was trying to kill Lewis. She wanted to rush at it and tear it to shreds. Was that what she was supposed to do, kill it? With the thing Mrs. Zimmermann had put in her hand? Or should she go straight to Lewis?

She didn't have long to make up her mind. Lewis's feet were touching the rock rim of the well. A slight push would send him plunging head first into darkness. With a loud screech Rose Rita ran forward. "Get away from him! Get away from him, don't you dare touch him, you filthy rotten thing!" she yelled.

The shadow turned and faced Rose Rita. And now it changed. Before, it had been a hooded, muffled shape. Now it was a ragged, spindly silhouette. A blackened,

shrunken corpse with living eyes. It moved toward her with outstretched, hungry arms. And Rose Rita heard what it was saying. She heard the words in her brain, although no sound was uttered. The thing was saying that it would wrap its arms around her and dive with her to the bottom of the dark, icy well. And there they would be, together, face to face, forever.

Rose Rita knew that if she thought, she would faint, or die. She clenched her teeth and rushed forward, saying over and over to herself the meaningless words of a commercial she had heard on the radio the other day. "Use Wildroot Cream Oil Charlie, use Wildroot Cream Oil Charlie, use . . ." The fearful shape rushed at her, and for a moment there was blackness all around her and the sickening, stifling smell of wet ashes. And then she was past it and standing by Lewis's side.

Lewis was actually teetering on the edge of the well. He had put one foot forward into nothingness, like somebody testing the water before he goes in. With a hard shove, Rose Rita pushed him sideways and back. Now her hands were around his neck, groping for the chain. Lewis did not resist. He acted like somebody who had been drugged. Still, it was hard for Rose Rita to get the chain off, because she had to hang onto the cold glowing object Mrs. Zimmermann had given her. She had a pretty good idea of what would happen to her if she let go of it.

With a jerk, Rose Rita pulled the chain up over Lewis's ears. She had it wadded in her hand now. When she turned toward the well, she saw the shape, muffled in darkness once again. It stood watching.

Rose Rita felt suddenly calm. Calm and triumphant.

"You see this?" she shouted, waving the amulet. *"Well, take a good look!"* And with that she flung the coin, chain and all, into the well.

There was a long second while the amulet fell. And then, from far below, came a tiny sound. *Plip.* And with that the dark hooded form vanished. It turned into a wisp of black smoke and was whipped away by the wind. Nothing was left, not even a smudge on the ground.

Rose Rita stood looking down into the well. It fascinated her. For a moment the well seemed like the only thing in the world. It was a great black whirlpool that would swallow her up. It was a dead eyesocket looking out of nothing into nothing. Rose Rita was caught in a sick convulsive shudder. She trembled from head to foot. But when she stopped trembling, her mind was clear. She stepped back from the edge of the well and turned to see if she could help Lewis.

Lewis was sitting on the ground crying. His face was red and raw from wind and snow and cold. His gloves were gone, his hat was gone, and there was a big piece torn out of his trouser leg. The first thing he said was, "Rose Rita, do you have a handkerchief? I have to blow my nose." Weeping with joy, Rose Rita threw her arms around Lewis and hugged him tight.

Now Jonathan and Mrs. Zimmermann were with them. They were crying too. But eventually Mrs. Zimmermann pulled herself together. She knelt down next to Lewis and started examining him like a doctor. She looked into his eyes, into his ears, and down his throat. She made him stick his tongue out and say "Aaah!" Jonathan and Rose Rita stood near, tense and nervous, waiting for Mrs. Zimmermann's verdict. Finally she stood up. She shook snow out of her cape and smoothed down her dress. "All that's wrong with *him*," she snorted, "is that he's been out in the weather too long. He's exhausted, and I think he has a cold. Rose Rita, would you hand me that thing I gave you?"

Suddenly Rose Rita remembered the object that had saved her. It was still in her hand, though it no longer glowed or felt cold. She opened her fist, and there was a glass tube about two inches long. Inside the tube was a perforated metal sleeve, and inside that were some pale violet crystals. On the end of the tube was a shiny gold-colored metal cap. There were words stamped into the top of the cap:

PEERLESS
Reg. U.S.
Pat. Off.
NASAL INHALATOR

Rose Rita turned to Mrs. Zimmermann. She didn't know whether to laugh or cry. "You mean that's all it was? One of those things you stick in your nose when your head is all stuffed up?"

"Yes, of course," said Mrs. Zimmermann, impatiently. "Now give it here. Thank you." As she worked over Lewis with the inhalator, Mrs. Zimmermann added: "It's also a magic object, the first one I ever made. And up until a minute ago, I thought the thing was a total flop. You see, it was made so it would only work if it was in the hands of a child. It was supposed to protect the child who used it from evil creatures. And it was supposed to have certain healing powers. Well, after I made it I lent it to a niece of mine in Muskegon, and she kept it for years. She's a grown-up woman now, and a few months ago she sent the thing back in a box with a little note saying that it was very good for clearing out a stuffy head, but that she didn't see anything magic about it. So I put the silly thing in a pocket of my cloak and forgot about it—until just now." Mrs. Zimmermann chuckled grimly. "I guess my niece just led a dull life. She never ran into anything like that dark shadow by the well."

Mrs. Zimmermann stood up and shook snow out of her cloak. Rose Rita looked down at Lewis, and she felt like cheering. Lewis looked dazed, but remarkably healthy. Now Mrs. Zimmermann turned to Rose Rita. She handed her the tube. "Here. Take it. It's yours. For good."

Tears came to Rose Rita's eyes. "Thanks. I hope I never have to use it the way I did tonight."

"So do I," said Mrs. Zimmermann.

"And I," said Jonathan, helping Lewis to his feet.

After Jonathan had made an unsuccessful attempt to get the lid back on the well, the four of them set out for the road. When they got there, they found an ambulance with its motor running. And there was Jute Feasel with Jonathan's car.

"Hi everybody!" Jute called. "I thought maybe you'd need this. I left my truck back where your car was, so if you'd drop me off there, I'd be obliged to you."

"It's a deal," Jonathan called, over his shoulder. He was talking with the ambulance driver, telling him that he wanted Lewis to spend the night in the hospital because he was suffering from cold and exposure. After that, Jonathan did a good deal of conferring with Mrs. Zimmermann, and in the end it was decided that she would ride back in the ambulance with Lewis, and the others would go back in Jonathan's car.

On the way back to New Zebedee, everybody in the car was silent for a long time. Jonathan drove, Jute rode next to him, and Rose Rita sat all by herself in the back. As they passed the CITY LIMITS sign, Jute spoke up. "I don't mean to be nosy, but what the he . . . oh hell, you don't mind if I swear, do you, Rose Rita? What the hell was Lewis doing out at the old Moss Farm in the middle of the night?"

Jonathan had begun a very hemmy and hawy explanation, when Rose Rita butted in. "It's all very simple, Mr. Feasel. What really happened was, Lewis was out walking by the city limits when this man he'd never seen before stopped in his car and asked him if he'd like to drive out to Homer and back, just to look at the snow. Well, Lewis does dumb things some of the time, and he said sure, and jumped in. But when they were halfway to Homer, the guy turned out to be one of these crazy people you read about in the papers, so Lewis jumped out of the car and hid in the woods. That was where we found him."

Jute puffed on his cigar and nodded. "Lewis get a good look at this guy?"

"No. It was dark. And he didn't get his license number, either. It's too bad. They'll probably never catch him."

"Yeah." Jute rode the rest of the way in silence. He did wonder how Jonathan and the others happened to know where to go to find Lewis. There weren't any telephones in that grove of pine trees. But Jute had heard that Jonathan was a magician, and maybe magicians had ways of communicating with people in their families. With brain waves or stuff like that. At any rate, Jute didn't ask any more questions, and Rose Rita rode the rest of the way home with a self-satisfied smile on her face.

/143/

CHAPTER THIRTEEN

Lewis woke up the next morning in a whitewashed room full of light. New Zebedee's hospital was in an enormous mansion that had once been owned by a rich old lady. Lewis's room was in the attic. The ceiling at the foot of his bed sloped down almost to the floor, and next to his elbow was a white plaster tunnel running out to a curtained dormer window at the end. Icicles hung outside, but it was warm in the room.

There were other patients in the long room, and nurses came and went all morning. Near noon, Dr. Humphries came to look Lewis over. He was the Barnavelts' family doctor, and Lewis liked him a lot. He had a voice like a bass viol, and he cracked jokes a lot to put people at their ease. And he always carried a black leather bag full of rattling square pill bottles. Dr. Humphries put a wooden stick in Lewis's mouth and flashed a light down his throat. He looked in his ears and eyes. Then he patted Lewis on the shoulder, snapped up his bag, and told him that a couple of days rest at home was all he needed. They shook hands, and Dr. Humphries left.

A few minutes later, Jonathan came to get Lewis, and they went home. Lewis was ordered to bed by Mrs. Zimmermann, and that evening, when she brought his supper up to him, she told him that she had a surprise: she and Jonathan and Rose Rita had arranged a special pre-Christmas Christmas party for him. He could put on his slippers and bathrobe and come down to the study as soon as he liked.

At first Lewis was frightened, because he had seen pictures in the paper of children who were dying of some incurable disease, like leukemia. They were always given early Christmas parties. But after Mrs. Zimmermann had reassured him several times that he wasn't on the brink of death, he felt better. In fact, he could hardly wait for the party to begin.

Lewis was sitting by the Christmas tree. He was looking at the red plaid Sherlock Holmes hat that Jonathan had bought to replace the one Woody had stolen. In one hand Lewis held a glass of Jonathan's special Christmas punch. In the other he held a chocolate-chip cookie.

This time he didn't have to squint to make the Christmas tree lights turn into stars. He was blinded by tears of happiness.

Rose Rita was sitting crosslegged on the floor near Lewis's armchair. She was playing with another of his presents, an electric pinball machine. "Mrs. Zimmermann?" she said.

"Yes, Rose Rita? What is it?" Mrs. Zimmermann was over by the library table, adding more Benedictine to her punch. Every year she claimed Jonathan went light on the Benedictine, and every year she doctored her drinks to suit herself. "Yes, my dear? What do you want?"

"When are you going to tell us how you figured out where to go? I mean, how you knew where Lewis was?"

Mrs. Zimmermann turned and smiled. She dipped her index finger in the punch, stirred, and put her finger in her mouth. "Mmm! Good! How did I know? Well, that's a good question. I thought over what you had told me about Lewis's experiences with the magic coin, and one detail kept ringing a bell in my mind. It was a detail that you probably didn't think was very important."

"Which one was that?" asked Lewis.

"The way the ghost smelled. Rose Rita said that you had told her the ghost smelled of wet ashes. It smelled like a fire that has just been put out. Well now, I put this fact together with a couple of others that I knew." Mrs.

Zimmermann held up a finger. "One: on the night of April 30, 1859, a farmer named Eliphaz Moss was burned to death in his farmhouse out near the Homer Road. My grandfather had a farm near there, and he was part of the bucket brigade that tried to put out the fire. When I was a child, I remember him telling me how awful it was to suddenly see old Eliphaz come tearing out of that house. He was all on fire. Then with a hideous screech (so my grandfather said) he threw himself into—"

"The well?" Lewis asked. His face had turned very pale.

"The well," said Mrs. Zimmermann, nodding grimly. "The well put the poor man's fire out, and it drowned him too. It's a very deep well, and they never recovered the body. Later, after the fire, somebody made a big, granite cover for the well, and the cover became Eliphaz's tombstone. That, by the way, is what your uncle is out doing now—helping Jute get the lid back on the well."

The front door slammed. It was Jonathan. When he came into the library, he was red-faced from the cold, but rather gloomy-acting. As soon as he had poured himself a cup of punch, he seemed more cheerful, so Mrs. Zimmermann went on with her story.

"Of course, that's only part of the tale," she said, pouring herself another cup of punch. "The second part concerns Walter Finzer, the man Grampa Barnavelt won the three-cent piece from. He was Eliphaz Moss's hired man, and everyone always believed that he had set the fire that killed old Eliphaz Moss."

"Why did they think that?" asked Rose Rita.

"Because Walter was a foul-tempered, nasty, cruel, lazy lout, that's why!" growled Jonathan. "Of course, you may have gathered that from the way he behaved when Grampa won his lucky piece."

"Do *you* think Walter Finzer set the fire, Mrs. Zimmermann?" It was Lewis this time asking the question.

"Yes," said Mrs. Zimmermann, nodding. "I didn't used to think so, but I do now. It's hard to piece things together from such little scraps and bits of evidence, but I'd say that Walter killed Eliphaz by knocking him unconscious and then setting fire to the house. By the time Eliphaz woke up, the house was on fire and he was, too."

"Why did Walter want to kill old Elly . . . whosis?" asked Rose Rita.

"To keep Eliphaz from getting back at him. You see, I think Walter stumbled into the house while Eliphaz was performing a magic ritual. Do you remember the date of the fire? April 30, 1859. Anybody remember anything special about April 30? You keep quiet, Jonathan. I know you know the answer."

Lewis thought a bit. "Hey!" he said. "That was the date on the newspaper that I saw just before the ghost came to get me. And 1859 was the date on the coin, too."

"That just makes me more certain than ever that my

theory is right," said Mrs. Zimmermann, smiling. "You see, April 30 is Walpurgis Night. It's sort of like Halloween—a night that is dear to the hearts of those who dabble in the black arts. Eliphaz dabbled in witchcraft, or at least, most of the farmers in the area thought he did. My grandfather thought so, for one." Mrs. Zimmermann stopped and stared into her glass. "You know," she said slowly, "it must have been awfully lonely on farms in those days. No TV, no radio, no car to take you into town for a movie. No movies at all. Farmers just kind of holed up for the winter. Some of them read the Bible, and some of them read—other books."

"You read those other books, too, don't you, Mrs. Zimmermann?" said Rose Rita in a small frightened voice.

Mrs. Zimmermann gave her a sour look. "Yes, I do, but I read them so I'll know what to do when something awful happens. And as you saw out there, sometimes it isn't enough to know about all these terrible books. Not when the other side's got more muscle."

"You're getting off the subject, Florence," said Jonathan. "So old Eliphaz was a wizard. Do you mean he was making the magic amulet when Walter burst in on him?"

"Yes. Walter probably came in for a plug of chewing tobacco or a drink of whiskey after a hard day's work. And there was Eliphaz doing some strange mumbo-jumbo over a little tiny silver coin. A three-cent piece. Well, everybody dreams about having a magic doohickey that will solve all their problems. The two men were alone out there, and Walter was probably by far the stronger. So Walter hit Eliphaz on the head, set fire to the house, and lit out—with the amulet. Then Walter must have decided that it would not be good for him to hang around New Zebedee. So he enlisted in the Army. Then the Civil War came along, Walter ran into Grampa Barnavelt—and you know the rest."

Lewis looked puzzled. "How come the ghost of old Eli . . . whatever-his-name-is was after me? Did he think I stole his amulet?"

"Not exactly," said Mrs. Zimmermann. "You see, the amulet was supposed to have the power to summon up a spirit from the depths. A spirit that would do Eliphaz Moss's bidding. But when you're fooling around with evil spirits, you've got to be careful, and the way I figure it, Eliphaz was interrupted before he had finished enchanting the coin. So things came out kind of screwy, as they would if you put the wrong ingredients in a cake you were making. And Eliphaz's spirit—his ghost, his soul, call it what you like—his spirit was the one called up when Lewis said the prayer from my book over the coin."

Lewis shuddered. "You mean I called him up? The ghost that smelled like ashes?"

Mrs. Zimmermann nodded. "You most certainly did. The prayer you said is what we professional wizards call a prayer of waking and possession. First, you woke up the spirit that had been asleep, the spirit that haunted the amulet—Eliphaz's spirit. The amulet couldn't do a thing to anybody until you recited that prayer. That is why Walter could never do anything with it, and was finally willing—albeit grudgingly—to toss it into the pot in a poker game. And that is also why Grampa Barnavelt could wear the coin on his belly for forty years and not be affected at all."

"But wait a minute," said Rose Rita. "I handled the coin after Lewis woke it up. How come nothing happened to me?"

"If you'll let me finish, I'll tell you why," said Mrs. Zimmermann patiently. "I said the prayer was a prayer of waking and *possession*. Lewis not only woke the amulet up, he made it his. His, and his alone. No one else could wield it. Of course, the amulet could be taken from him by force—as it was—but no one else could do anything with it. It was his until it was destroyed. I don't know whether you realize it, Rose Rita, but you wiped out the enchantment that had been laid on the coin when you dropped it into the well. Water is the cleansing element, the element of rebirth. It wipes out all curses. Running water is best, but good old stagnant well water is okay, too. That's why the dark shape vanished when it did. The enchantment was over."

"I still don't see why old what-sis-name was after me," said Lewis.

Mrs. Zimmermann sighed. "Well, there again, we can

only guess. Eliphaz was trying to make an amulet of power. Amulets of power can be used to call up spirits —usually evil ones—and they can give the owner of the amulet wonderful powers. Simon Magus owned an amulet of power, and it is said that he could fly through the air and make himself invisible."

"Do they help you win fights?" asked Lewis in a weak little voice.

Mrs. Zimmermann chuckled. "Yes, they do. Eliphaz's ghost helped you win that fight with Woody. Eliphaz had been trapped into being the spirit of his own amulet— sort of like a genie in a jug, if you see what I mean. Well, he had to obey the rules. You summoned him, and he gave you power. But then, as time passed, Eliphaz's spirit began to take shape in this world. At first he only sent you messages to let you know he was coming— postcards and the like. Finally, he took on the form you saw under the street lamp, and in the shadows under the arch of the Masonic Temple. Well now, Lewis, if you had been a wizard, there would have been no problem. You would have tamed the spirit. You would have made Eliphaz carry out your commands. But you were just a little boy who didn't know what he was doing, so Eliphaz decided to turn the tables and carry you off to his . . . his home." Mrs. Zimmermann shuddered and stopped talking. She stared hard at the fire. She was thinking about the well and what was in it.

Everyone sat silent, and for a few minutes it looked as if it was going to be a very gloomy Christmas party. But then Jonathan cleared his throat loudly and announced that, seeing as how it was Christmas for Lewis, it might as well be Christmas for everybody.

"You mean we all get to open our presents?" said Rose Rita. She sounded very excited.

Jonathan nodded. "That is exactly what I mean. Come on, everybody. Dive in!"

Before long the floor of the study was awash in a sea of colored paper. Mrs. Zimmermann got a new umbrella to replace the one that had been destroyed in her duel with Eliphaz Moss's ghost. This new umbrella was not magic, but she said she would get to work on it soon. Jonathan got his usual seven or eight pounds of tobacco, and a meerschaum pipe carved in the shape of a dragon. The smoke was supposed to come out through the dragon's nose and mouth. Rose Rita got a fielder's mitt and a season ticket for four to the Detroit Tigers' home games in the coming season. Jonathan and Mrs. Zimmermann were both baseball fans, and they were always arguing, since Jonathan liked the Tigers and Mrs. Zimmermann liked the White Sox. Jonathan grinned with delight when he thought of how many times the four people in this room would be going to baseball games in the coming year. And Rose Rita would get to take them all, since it was her ticket.

The party went on for hours until finally everyone was so tired they could hardly keep their eyes open. Rose Rita and Mrs. Zimmermann went home, and the other two dragged themselves off to bed.

Several days later, Lewis was in the front hall tugging at a boot that just would not go on. Suddenly the mail slot flapped, and a smooth white packet fell onto the doormat. At first, Lewis was terrified. But then, after he had calmed down, he hobbled over to the door and picked the envelope up. Lewis started to laugh. It was the Charles Atlas booklet.

About the Author

John Bellairs was the critically acclaimed, best-selling author of many Gothic novels: *The Curse of the Blue Figurine, The Mummy, the Will, and the Crypt, The Lamp from the Warlock's Tomb, The Spell of the Sorcerer's Skull, The Revenge of the Wizard's Ghost, The Chessmen of Doom, The Eyes of the Killer Robot,* and the novels starring Lewis Barnavelt, Rose Rita Pottinger, and Mrs. Zimmermann—*The House with a Clock in Its Walls, The Figure in the Shadows, The Letter, the Witch, and the Ring,* and *The Ghost in the Mirror* (completed by Brad Strickland).

John Bellairs died in 1991. However, there are several more books that Mr. Bellairs left that Puffin will be publishing. Brad Strickland, a longtime Bellairs fan, will be completing them, just as he did *The Ghost in the Mirror*.

About the Artist

Mercer Mayer is the creator of many acclaimed picture books, including the classic *There's a Nightmare in My Closet, There's an Alligator Under My Bed,* and *There's Something in My Attic.* He and his wife and children share their Connecticut farm with a dog, a cat, and four horses.